HUNTING WITH DINOSAURS

DOUG GOODMAN

SEVERED PRESS
HOBART TASMANIA

HUNTING WITH DINOSAURS

ISBN: *978-1-922551-54-2*

"Fish," he said, "I love you and respect you very much. But I will kill you dead before this day ends."
-Ernest Hemingway, The Old Man and the Sea

Forgive your enemy, but remember the bastard's name.
-Scottish proverb

PART ONE: RULES OF PREDATION

The aim of life was meat. Life itself was meat. Life lived on life. There were the eaters and the eaten. The law was: EAT OR BE EATEN. He did not formulate the law in clear, set terms and moralize about it. He did not even think the law; he merely lived the law without thinking about it at all.

— Jack London, White Fang

I do not know the way the hearth-light burns
Nor how the kiss of childish lips may feel,
I only know the way the mad sea churns
And how the blowing spray, like bits of steel,
Can tear like savage teeth, and rip from me,
These last reluctant hopes, and leave me free.

-Louis L'amour, The Wanderer

CHAPTER ONE

This was our last attempt to kill the dinosaurs. They'd eluded us for days. Everything seemed against us, even the damn mountains. The misshapen peaks and broken ridgelines of the Perdidos Mountains were an angry circle glaring with all their weight down upon us puny mortals. The cold wind stiffened our spines. Our boots slumped in wet snow, entombing them in ice. God, have you hiked in wet snow? It is a bitter, brittle battle between your self-heat and the cold outside. Of all the places I've hunted, this wilderness was the most uninviting.

Jan carried a Remington 700 rifle, Mad Dog laid metal on the ground. The last man in line was me; I volunteered to sherpa the deer carcass, shouldering it over my pack while the others carried my bow and arrows. We decided to change tactics, and rather than pursue them, we'd lure them to us with the dead deer. The problem was, it worked. Now we were being hunted by the dinosaurs.

We studied the trees like a group of soldiers behind enemy lines. We dissected the sounds of cracking branches and took telemetry from the movement of leaves in the air. We read shadows the way farmers transcribed storms and droughts from cloud formations and beetle populations.

"Are they coming to us?" Jan asked. He was the tallest one of us. A veritable giant. He was also twenty-five years older than me and Mad Dog. He looked through his Leupold scope, which cast a ghostly green gleam across his face, like he was some futuristic terminator scanning the trees for aliens. "I want a good shot."

"Don't worry, Jan. You'll get yer trophy," Mad Dog grunted. To this day, I don't know Mad Dog's real name. Though Jan was older, Mad Dog seemed like he stepped out of a different era, or perhaps even another world. He dropped something large and metallic into the path behind the three hunters. "And I'll get my beastie."

"We shouldn't be using traps," I said, shifting the weight of the dead deer on my shoulders. The deer was packed into an old body bag so as not to cover me in blood. The not-yet-frozen blood sloshed, pooling at the bottom of the bag. I wasn't thinking of the blood, though. I watched in bewilderment as Mad Dog set up his steel trap. "If you're not careful, Mad Dog, we won't need this damn deer carcass that Jan shot."

"Don't worry your pretty head. I'm always careful with my traps."

"Those traps are illegal in California."

Mad Dog pried the steel jaws apart until they snapped into position. He'd already hammered the pin into the ground beneath the snow. "Well, the sheriff gave me permission because the way he sees it, those laws are for mammals and say nothing of dinosaurs."

I remembered Sheriff Castillo. He was a tall man with a round face and a sense of proprietary justice that was as uncompromising as the Perdidos. The good sheriff reminded me of a lord ruling over his lands, and his words rang in my ears.

"I've summoned you three here because I know you to be excellent hunters," Sheriff Castillo said, "and I want these monsters killed before the Federals or Big Pharma finds out. *Hijole.* The last thing this county needs is to be overrun by Government agents and company reps who will likely live-trap the damned things and return them to Dinosaur Falls. I want you to kill these monsters and get justice for the children's parents."

"Dinosaurs wouldn't have this problem if they stayed in their area," Jan added. "Dinosaur Falls National Restricted Area has been around for more than ten years. Nobody's allowed inside except rangers. The only way to see the dinosaurs is through cameras, right? Well, that is what they want you to think. Despite what the government claims, people have seen these resurrected monsters attacking their cattle and running off with their livestock. I've heard stories."

Mad Dog winked. "Right, Jan. If you got a problem with traps, Cody, go back to LA."

"I just don't want to go to jail."

Trap in place, Mad Dog lowered his head to the steel teeth a little too close for my comfort level. Mad Dog eyeballed the path into the clearing where we were making camp for the night.

"Trust me, you ain't goin' to jail for this. These Velociraptors escaped that restricted area and killed some kids. They got what's coming to them. This ain't no ethical kill either. Just put the monsters down, and Sheriff Castillo will give you a gold medal and the key to the county."

As if to answer Mad Dog, a high-pitched shriek pierced the dark trail behind us. The sound was like nothing else I'd heard before. Imagine an eagle screaming while simultaneously being struck by lightning. The shriek was a blasphemy in the natural world, a reminder that these creatures hadn't walked North America since it was part of a supercontinent millions of years ago.

The screech left a void in its wake, as if no animal dared follow it. Five seconds later, an eerie second electric cry broke out, but to the right of the first one.

"Good. They's coming," Mad Dog said. A hidden smile appeared in his long, shaggy beard.

"I need to set up my blind," Jan said. "We need to lay out the carcass before they arrive."

Ritual is important to hunters. I think that's where people misunderstand hunters. Killing an animal, as part of a hunt, is no flippant errand. Hunting the right way is a long line of procedures that begins with background checks and licenses and property rentals and scheduling arrangements and ends with a weapon drawn, a projectile loaded, and finally, the release. All these processes encourage rituals. Rituals a hunter stands by.

For example, Jan set up his blind in a very specific way. I'd seen him set it up three times already. He only did it the one way. He always dropped his pack to the left of where he built the blind, and every time, he propped his long rifle against a tree to the left of his pack. He tied orange flagging tape to the end of his barrel. ("You only lose a rifle in the woods once," he muttered the first time he set up his blind.) Rifle, pack, blind. It never varied. It was his ritual.

Once he placed his equipment where he wanted it, you'd think he would start building the blind, right? No. First, Jan looked up, down, left, and right. I thought of dogs turning in a spot before laying down. I wondered if I called out from his right before he could turn left, would I set him off? Would he go up, down, right, left, right? I didn't want to be cruel. We all have our process.

Even Mad Dog followed a ritual. He always looked up and down the lines of passage after setting his trap. (There's a lot of looking in our rituals, I admit. Probably because of gun sighting.)

Me, I rolled my arrows across my forearm to check for any faults. I checked my compound bow and its strings to ensure their strength. I strapped on my neon pink-camo leather bracer and slid my middle fingers into my finger tab, flexing my fingers three times. I've checked the same arrow dozens of times in the span of a week, and I still do it. It's good practice, but a little OCD.

"Can I ask you something?" Mad Dog asked while watching me. (Perhaps he was pondering my rituals.)

"Sure."

"I've always been interested in bow hunting. Me and my Daddy, though, we never hunted that way. We was always into trappin' and shootin'. I tell you that 'cause I don't want you to think I'm completely stupid when it comes to huntin', I just don't know much about bows and arrows."

"You want to know how it works?"

"Well, kinda. Yeah. I mean, I've shot a bow and arrow. I've just never hunted with one, you know?"

I held out the bow to him, and he examined it. The blue-and-gray bridge was thin and lightweight, with black fiberglass upper and lower limbs.

"With all them bowstrings, how do you know which one to use? It looks like a spider playing little kids' string games."

"I hadn't thought about it that way. I guess it does. My Mom taught me playing those games as a kid. I don't think I could do them again."

"Why so many strings?"

"Well, actually, it's one string, the bowstring, and two cables in front of it. The cables create power while reducing the draw."

"Draw? You mean when you pull back?"

I nodded. "Every bow has a different draw strength. Higher draw strength, more power. Also, the farther you can shoot an arrow. Most people use a thirty to fifty-pound bow for hunting. This one is seventy pounds because I'd rather overkill a dinosaur than have the arrow bounce off."

"Wow, man. You're like Hawkeye, ain't ya?" Mad Dog asked while handing the bow back.

"He is John Rambo!" Jan teased from within the blind.

I laughed perfunctorily. I wasn't a superhero or a super soldier. I wasn't a super anything. Unlike every fictional character ever, I was a decent shot, but I'd never been a great shot. My strengths were that I was diligent and persistent. I didn't give up on a kill.

"Rambo! Hoorah!" Mad Dog said with a laugh.

Jan said, "I tried bow hunting once. I didn't have the strength for it. I'm not built like you."

I held up a small purple piece of metal curved to fit my fingers. "Thanks for the compliment, but the cables keep the weight low. And I practice a lot."

While Jan and I finished building our perches and conducting our rituals, Mad Dog set up his dome tent.

"Hardest animal to kill," he said, "And Go!" Like he was posting his challenge to the Internet.

"Bison are tough. Mountain goats are tricky," I threw out there.

"Not lions?"

I was about to say no, then I changed my mind. "Well, I wasn't on a trophy hunt. Those lions were harassing the village."

"Coyotes ain't lions, but they're some of the most mistrusting creatures on God's earth. They're as likely to dig up my trap as they are to avoid it, and when I have caught one, they'd leave me nothing but a bloody stump to show for all my work."

"I've heard tales of how elusive coyotes can be," I said.

"What do you think, Jan? We're hunting raptors here. What animal's toughest?" Mad Dog asked the oldest hunter, who had been quiet up until this point.

Jan scoffed from behind his blind. "None of them."

"The great white hunter, ladies and gents," Mad Dog intoned.

Jan put down the pole he was manipulating. "No animal is so strong that it cannot be stopped by a bullet. Killing an animal is easy. Aim and pull the trigger. Any hunter who can hit a target from 40 yards can kill just about any animal in the world, dinosaurs included. The hard part is finding the animal and bringing it to you. Hunting is hard. Shooting is easy."

"Amen, brother," Mad Dog said.

When his tent was finally up, Mad Dog announced, "I'm going to find some firewood."

"No fire," Jan ordered. "You'll ward them off."

"Without a fire I'll freeze my butt cheeks to the ground. I'm not up in a warm tree or behind a blind like you two."

"Yes, but you are sleeping in a sleeping bag that should be certified for freezing temperature, or you're a fool. No fire." Jan had the Nordic clip of somebody born in the Netherlands who had immigrated to the States. At first, it was a little off-putting, but after a couple days in the backwoods, I grew fond of his brusqueness. He never held anything back. I always knew where I stood with him.

Mad Dog grumbled, but went back about his business.

After nightfall we waited for the dinosaurs to approach. The dead deer, a buck, lay on the snowy ground between us and the edge of the clearing. We made sure to lay the buck so that its scent carried to the animal trail. This would lure the walking monstrosities.

The full moon rose over the mountains. "That's a January Moon," I said. "A Wolf Moon."

5

"Yes," Jan said from down behind his blind. He said *Yes* as the end of a conversation, not the start. The time for camaraderie and small talk was over. We were hunting now. The Wait. The three of us remained still and quiet. We tuned our ears to the sounds of pine needles falling and wind whistling. Even in the dead of winter, the mountains reverberated with the music of the forest.

A few coyotes howled at the moon. I'd heard many coyotes and wolves howling during my hunting career. I often wondered, if wolf howls could ever be translated to speech, what would they say? To me, they always sounded like sad and lonely songs. Dirges to dead lovers or lost lives.

I thought of the Sheriff's deputy, an old man named Keeler, who led our excursion to the Calavera River County Park. He wasn't happy about it, either. "What's bothering you, old timer?" Jan asked after we'd all exited our trucks and geared up for the hunt.

The color drained from Deputy Keeler's face. "You're all out of your God-DAMNED minds to go out in this weather hunting those monsters. They come from Dinosaur Falls, you know, and it's a restricted area for good reason. Eighty percent of everyone who has ever been dumb enough to enter that area without a damn army behind 'em has been killed by a dinosaur. Why you three want to take on those odds I'll never understand."

"Eighty percent weren't us," Jan said.

"No, you're right. Eighty percent were professional outdoorsmen and women who knew what they were doing. You're just men with guns. Guns have never stopped a dinosaur before."

"Beg your pardon," I said, "but we aren't going to Dinosaur Falls."

Noticing me as if for the first time, the old deputy reached for my throat. A small silver-and-black Celtic cross hung around my neck.

"Prayer won't help you. You're hunting perhaps the smartest, most malicious hunter that has ever walked the Earth. You've seen the documentaries. Velociraptors are surplus killers. That means they kill more than they will ever eat. Velociraptors aren't bears or lions that may see you as a threat and run. Velociraptors don't fear humans at all! The thousands of years of humans hunting bears and lions hasn't happened to raptors. They'll kill you just to bring you down, then walk away like it was nothing. Look, I'm bringing you here because I was ordered to. Once you take two steps in there, it's not on my conscience. I've done everything I can to dissuade you."

"This ain't on you, brother," Mad Dog said. "We got a job to do. We aim to do it. See, we're professionals, too. But we's pro-fessional killers."

"You're fools, all fools. But I've said my piece. I'll only say this one last thing, something to think about before you enter that trail." He stopped and faced me squarely. "You are entering the wilderness area adjacent to Dinosaur Falls. The average lifespan of somebody entering that area is 44 hours. Not even two full days. Keep that countdown clock in the back of your mind while you're hunting in the backcountry."

Without another word, Deputy Keeler and his ominous warnings climbed into his Sheriff's Department patrol car and drove away.

***

We sensed the emergence of the raptors and searched the darkness in the pines. Three sets of eyes reflected in the moonlight. My skin wanted to jump off my skeleton. These blank eyes, avian and reptilian at the same time, they didn't blink, but stared at us, lusting for our meat. They floated like ghosts in the dark. The eyes remained at the edge of the tree line.

Jan raised his Remington 700. Slowly, he adjusted his sight. "Oh, they're magnificent," Jan said. "They're staying at the edge of the clearing. There are three of them."

I couldn't see them as easily. My bow didn't have a nightscope. But every once in a while, a head bobbed above the creamy moonlit snow. Rough scaly skin like the feet of a hawk, sharp teeth, and taut, wiry muscles. These bodies rippled with power, like slings pulled tight and begging to be released.

All at once, the trap snapped, the Velociraptors screamed, and the Remington boomed. The black trees shook in the moonlight. Snow fluttered from the branches. Then came the tap dance rhythm of the cartridge being ejected from the bolt action and a new one chambered as the bolt closed the breech. I'd heard the melody often in my time. The automation of the sound was comforting in an oddly Pavlovian way.

The casing made a soft thwip! as it fell into the snow below.

"Did you get one?" I asked, my tone perhaps a little overeager, a reflection of the bolt action's tap dance.

"No," Jan said. "Damn. I thought I had it."

Once the wilderness grew quiet and still again and we were sure the Velociraptors weren't close, we plodded out to the trap through the crunching snow.

"Do you think they'll be back?" Mad Dog asked. "I hope you didn't scare them off."

Jan said, "Everything we've ever heard of raptors dictates that they will return."

We entered the forest path. Up ahead lay a tussle of broken snow, sans the metal trap.

"How did they get it?" Mad Dog asked. His voice changed an octave with incredulity. Even I had to balk at the sight. Those traps constrained the mightiest apex predators.

"Did you see?" Mad Dog asked Jan.

Jan shook his head. "I was too busy shooting to watch what else they were doing. Sorry."

"Cody?"

My head swayed side to side.

Mad Dog checked the hole in the ground where he'd planted the trap. "Are they really strong enough to pull the bolt? These bolts're strong enough to hold a tiger."

"Chalk it up to one more lesson learning to hunt dinosaurs. There's so much we don't know about these things," I said.

"Maybe not you," Jan said, "but like a good hunter, I study my quarry, these Utahraptors. They're not Velociraptors as you keep calling them, Mad Dog. I've watched over a hundred hours of these Utahraptors on the video feeds from the restricted area. I'm not as ignorant as the deputy claimed."

"And what'd it teach you?" I asked.

"Like you, Cody, I've hunted most animals that can kill you. After a while, you get used to their lack of ethics. I once saw a lion eat the anus out of a water buffalo. It never let go, and eventually, the buffalo died. Carnivores will use any tactic they can to kill because their bodies require meat to survive. To call one animal good or evil is to ignore its base nature. It anthropomorphizes them, right? But raptors? They're pure evil."

"You got that right, Jan," Mad Dog said. "They took off with my trap. Do you know how much that thing costs? I only got four left."

In the distance, a Utahraptor's painful wail burned through the night. Each one of us felt that monster's emotion in our weary bones, and it made us anxious of their retaliation.

"I think we better light that fire now," Mad Dog suggested.

"Sure," I said, more spooked than I was willing to admit. We were great hunters after all. We couldn't be scared of our prey.

CHAPTER TWO

Glowing dimly in the firelight, the deer now dangled upside down in the tree. We weren't worried about bears. In winter's abyss, they were all in deep hibernation. In fact, only one animal seemed to not have sense to escape the frigid cold of winter. I thought about how, years ago, I'd read that dinosaurs use air sacs and blood flow to stay warm in the coldest months.

The Utahraptors wailed throughout the night. Heavy metal banshees. None of us caught any sleep. We tossed inside our sleeping bags. The wailing went on and on into the midnight hours until I couldn't tell when one scream ended and another began. It was as infinite as the night. And always was the question, are they getting closer?

My mind played tricks on me the deeper I ventured into the night. Every twenty minutes I would be certain that a raptor's voice was so close its twisted form would appear as a shadow on my tent. The only shapes on the tent were the gnarled fingers of the tree embellished by the firelight. But those fingers didn't help me to sleep, either. I imagined Death approaching once more, his ugly fingers dancing with glee as he neared my still-breathing corpse.

I volunteered for the first watch, then Mad Dog took the watch after me, then finally Jan. And yet I was awake for every changing of the guard. If not for Jan's whistling, which acted as a kind of noise machine lulling me into a different section of my brain, I never would have gotten to sleep.

***

The next morning, Mad Dog woke me with a groan.

"I need coffee like nobody's business," he said from inside his tent.

"I'd like to order another ten hours of sleep," I said like I was requesting breakfast and he was my waiter, and sleep was on the menu.

Mad Dog chuckled. I turned over in my bag. The cold pressed against my sleeping bag's warmth. I fought it, knowing it was a battle I'd eventually lose. Inevitably, I'd have to get up.

I listened to Mad Dog scrounging around in his tent and shoving his feet in his boots. Then came the metal whine of his tent flaps's zipper.

Zzzzrrrrrrzzzziiiiip! The flap beat against his tent. I could feel the cold wind pressing against Mad Dog. Empathically, I curled into my pillow tighter.

"Cody!"

The nascent alarm in his voice goaded me out of my bag. "What is it?" I asked, even though something wet was trickling through the back of my mind. An acknowledgement, perhaps, of the vast absence of sound filling up the morning. No baleful wails. No crunching footsteps. No crackling fire. No coffee percolating on coals. And before the words came out of Mad Dog's mouth, I knew.

"Jan is gone."

"Gone? What do you mean?"

"He ain't here."

My mind grasped for a logical explanation, something with sound reasoning. Quickly, I formed an idea.

"He probably just went to take a leak." That made perfect sense. *I've got to test my handwriting. I need to stream, nature-style. I need to find a tree.* All euphemisms for the same biological necessity, one that somehow grew funnier and more indulgent any time men shared the wilderness together. There is a mathematical model out there that predicts the ratio of pissing euphemisms to the length of time spent outdoors.

Jan had to take a piss. That was the simple answer. Order was restored to the world in a yellow stream.

"I don't think so. Come look." His words were tinged with despair.

I jammed on my boots and my fleece and clambered outside on hands and feet. No matter how cool the outdoorsman, we all fumble out of our tents like newborn deer being birthed.

The icy dryness slapped me in the face, stinging my cheeks. The bite of the cold did not compare to the pained shock of seeing Jan's tent shredded.

"Jesus," I exclaimed. A red smear ran a line out of Jan's tent and off into the woods. I thought of a kid's crayon drawn along the white paper of the snowfall. I remembered another time I stood in the woods surrounded by human blood.

Mad Dog said, "That's insane. I ain't never seen an animal just drag a hunter off like that. Not without making a sound. What do we do?"

At first I didn't hear him. I was lost in my vision, but quickly I came back.

Bloody trail leading into the bushes? Let me assure you, I know that common sense would be to turn tail and run. My first instinct was to do my best impression of Forest Gump out of the mountains. But I was a hunter, and Jan was my comrade. So I had to do the mental version of swallowing a gulp in my throat and do the right thing.

"We're hunters," I said. "We follow the trail."

***

Mad Dog wanted to disagree, but he couldn't find a good enough reason not to. Following trails, especially bloody trails, was what we did. This was not the way we wanted the hunt to go, but they were the cards we'd drawn. I couldn't help thinking of the old deputy's words and his timeline. We made it three days instead of two, but we weren't in Dinosaur Falls either, were we?

"Guess you're right. Belly-aching won't do anything about it," Mad Dog said. "Did he at least leave his rifle?"

Mad Dog and I quickly climbed into the rest of our clothes and grabbed our weapons. Breaking camp could wait for later.

I scrounged through Jan's belongings, searching for his Remington and a clue for why the raptors attacked. In my experience, animals rarely initiated aggression on a human in their tent. Animals entered tents hunting leftover food or some other smelly thing. Jan's tent was clean, however. No snacks and no heavily scented items.

"His rifle is missing."

Mad Dog cursed under his breath.

I grabbed my compound bow and my quiver, and we followed the blood trail across the snowfield and into the trees. At the edge of the trees, I said, "He was still alive when they dragged him through here."

Mad Dog's eyes fell on the trees and dry brush. Branches were soaked in blood. Broken fingernails scratched at rocks. Jan struggled for his life. Why didn't he call out for help?

I led with my arrows. Mad Dog pulled a gut hook knife, a slick one. As the name implies, a thick hook jutted backwards along the spine of the fixed blade. The blade stretched out from a textured deer horn handle. Ten minutes later, we found what was left of Jan's body.

"Gawd," Mad Dog said. "Ain't nothin' left of him."

We set out investigating the kill site. We'd both encountered similar situations, having trailed felled quarry only to discover the animal attacked and eaten by a bear or mountain lion. Just as in those cases, there was a story to discover here. While Mad Dog canvassed the surrounding area, I concentrated on Jan's body.

The poor man's throat was slit across the front. His larynx was destroyed. Not lacerated but destroyed. The gash had nearly decapitated him. He didn't live more than three seconds after that cut. No wonder we never heard him cry out.

I made the sign of the cross.

"What?" Mad Dog asked.

"A Utahraptor must've slit his throat with one of their giant claws. Look at that damage. The claw literally demolished his larynx. He bled out from this wound. There really isn't a lot of blood elsewhere."

"'Cause it's all back on the trail behind us."

"What?"

"The Remington's destroyed." Then Mad Dog added, "We should get outta here."

"Why?"

"Can't you hear it? The silence?"

I hadn't been thinking of anything but the impromptu autopsy in front of me. Now that I was paying attention, I heard the nothing, too.

"That's us. This is a kill site. Kill sites have ways of driving off prey animals."

Mad Dog said, "Right, but this is different. Didn't Jan say that these raptors were particularly...evil? The deputy practically said it, too."

"So?"

"And we left bait out for them last night."

I finally caught up with Mad Dog's train of thought. My eyes scanned the ground in front of us. I didn't notice any signs to warn me that raptors were waiting to ambush us, but I also knew that this was how people got killed.

We backed away from the kill site. As we retreated, I stopped Mad Dog and pointed to the ground. "Boot steps."

"Yours?"

"Jan's." I pointed into the distance. "They goaded him into running. They were toying with him. God knows how he tried to run. Once he was running, they dragged him back." My voice as bottomless as the darkest hole in the ground, I added, "For fun."

"I really don't wanna be here anymore," Mad Dog said.

We watched our peripherals while retracing our steps back to camp. And yeah, we ran the last twenty yards.

"Let's get our gear and go," Mad Dog said.

Unfortunately, the raptors had different plans for us. The camp was trashed, our tents destroyed. Deer antlers pointed up from within the crumpled ruins of one of the tents.

"They ate the deer, too? Jesus Christ," Mad Dog exclaimed.

Pulling back the rain fly, I said, "No, they didn't consume it. They tore it out of the tree and threw it on our tents. See? No bites and no tears on the carcass. Just Jan's gunshot wound."

"What the hell's wrong with these things? Let's radio the Sheriff's department."

"We haven't had service in three days, and you know it. The Perdidos block all the signals."

"I was hoping maybe you could get a link." His pallid face begged me to try my cell.

We both pulled our smartphones out of our packs and turned them on, then waited futilely until the NO SERVICE notation appeared.

I turned the phone off and tossed it back into my pack, muttering, "Useless as a brick." To Mad Dog, I said, "Let's go. Leave what you can spare. With any luck, we can be back in the parking lot by nightfall."

A lonely electric wail echoed off the mountain rocks.

"Cody? How far away do you think that thing is?"

"Maybe two miles if we're lucky. Then again, it was here while we were investigating Jan's body. It could be another one's closer."

That's all the motivation we needed. We slapped our gear into the bags with little care and less organization, and then we began the long hike out. For five tough hours, we packed through the mountains, which seemed to fight us every step of the way. Or maybe it was just because Mad Dog insisted on a more direct route that took us through deeper snow. Our calves disappeared into the white. It's as if we were being erased from the world.

We stopped in the early afternoon only because we were forced to eat and rest. Our stomachs rumbled. We were expending calories like Olympic swimmers. Our icy breath plumed between mouthfuls of beef jerky and naan bread.

When Mad Dog spoke, he broke a silence that had enveloped us for the past five hours.

"We're not making miles," Mad Dog huffed. "These mountains is against us. We ain't gonna make it. At least not tonight."

"That's not the worst part."

"They're following us?"

I nodded.

Mad Dog looked around. "I was wondering why the bastards weren't screeching."

"They're sneaky, staying just out of reach from us. I spotted one. It had an ugly face."

"How ugly?"

"Well, did you ever hear of the comic book character named Jonah Hex?"

"I remember the movie."

"Well, one of our pursuers has a face like that. Half of it is melted off."

We hiked the rest of the day, but we didn't get much farther in the cold Perdidos Mountains. Jagged rocks clawed out of the snow like zombies from their graves. They bit and grabbed at our ankles and slowed our pace. We kept slipping on other rocks and falling, busting our hands on stones hidden in the snow. And with every fall, I expected one of those three raptors, perhaps Jonah himself, to jump out of the trees and attack us. That fear motivated us.

It was some of the worst backpacking I've ever experienced.

By four in the afternoon, it was apparent we needed to make camp and prepare for the long night. Being the middle of winter, the sun would be down before six, and there was a lot of work to complete if we were going to survive the night.

First, Mad Dog set all five of his traps in the surrounding forest. While he worked the traps, I worked on the fire. Fire had protected us the night before. Hopefully it would protect us again tonight. I used my camping axe to hack large branches from the trees. I dug a narrow trench and moved most of the snow out of the way. Now I needed something to shield the bottom of the fire from the wet ground.

Luckily, I'd spotted some birch trees earlier. They were rare in this part of California. I scraped the bark off stowed them in my pack. Now I placed the ribbons of bark on the bottom of the trench, then I erected a series of pyramid fires in a row, all on top of each other. The trench was three feet deep and ten feet long.

While I positioned the branches, Mad Dog gathered tinder. Dry leaves were nowhere to be found, but pine needles were abundant, and they stayed dry even in the snow. He collected great bunches of pine needles and dumped them into the pyramids. While he gathered tinder, he was stopped by a wolf's distant howl.

"Damn this winter," Mad Dog cursed, looking at the Wolf Moon rising low in the west. "I swear, that sun barely rose."

He hustled back to camp, scared that one of the Utahraptors might take him while we were separated. I couldn't say he was wrong. We'd both debated the safety of separating more than a few feet from each other, but we decided that if the raptors were still around and wanted to kill us, they would have done it already. For whatever reason, they were leaving us alone. Perhaps they preferred to attack at night.

We didn't pitch our tents but slept under the clear night sky. Mad Dog and I watched the moon rise and wondered what terrors the night would bring. We'd both been tested many times before we ever walked into the Perdidos Mountains, but when I looked into Mad Dog's eyes, I saw my fear reflected in him, and I saw my face in his bright black eyes, and I was very scared. Would we live to see the sunrise? I wasn't sure.

And then the raptors attacked.

CHAPTER THREE

I spotted them first. "Don't react. They're standing fifty yards out. All three are ahead of us."

My gut tightened. I'd never seen dinosaurs "in the flesh." In the past, I didn't have a big impression one way or the other about dinosaurs. Sure, I'd seen the documentaries and the YouTube channels. I'd even watched a couple of compilations from live feeds. Who wouldn't? But alive and in front of my eyes, I had a whole other outlook on them. It was pretty simple, too. Oh, they should all be killed.

The raptors reminded me of Xenomorphs and gray-skinned alien monsters. Their skin was rough, and their body was muscular. Athletic. But they clearly did not belong here. This went way beyond invasive species. Invasive species are a blasphemy of geography and location. These creatures were a desecration of time.

Jonah towered over the other two raptors, one of which had a bloated, wormy gut. They weren't hiding at all. They stood boldly in the open, like there was no creature on Earth that could stop them. They stared with eyes that weren't quite reptilian, but something more than an eagle's.

Mad Dog growled, "Good. I dropped three traps out there." To the raptors, he yelled, "Come ON IN!"

"If they weren't drawn in by a fresh kill, I doubt taunting will work."

Mad Dog ignored me. He turned around and dropped his pants and wiggled his bare white ass to the raptors. "Nice and TAY-steee!"

I laughed, but I lit the fire. I wanted flames between me and these things. A parenthesis of flame spread between us and the dinosaurs. Behind us was a cliff. We couldn't be outflanked, which was good. Then again, we'd trapped ourselves with no way out. We were literally with our backs against the wall.

Once the fire was burning bright, the Utahraptors disappeared into the shadows. I couldn't believe how fast they sprinted. I'd seen them running in videos, but in person they were so much faster!

Snap!

Snap!

Snap!

The traps were sprung. I wasn't ready to celebrate, but it was a good sign.

Loud, bird-like noises scratched the night air. Their vocalizations were like the sounds light bulbs make before they burst.

"Gotcha, you hellhounds!" Mad Dog yelled. He hadn't stopped waving his naked ass at them.

Before Mad Dog could finish his expletives, three traps flew through the flames and landed in the snow in front of us. One bounced off the cliffside behind us.

"That's impossible," Mad Dog said, jerking up his pants. His traps were bent and broken. "That's iron. They can't bend solid iron."

I didn't know what to tell Mad Dog. I was just as perplexed. "I'm starting to think the usual laws of nature don't apply to raptors."

"Ha!"

Since I didn't have an answer, I searched the trees, hoping to catch at least a glimpse of our attackers. I couldn't focus on anything beyond the firelight.

Mad Dog moaned and groused as his hands worked over his traps, like he was trying to find a way to convince them to unbend.

"They don't make traps like this anymore. My granddaddy trapped in Oregon with these babies."

I waited ten long minutes for the Utahraptors to continue their attack, but they never reappeared. This should've made me feel better, but it had just the opposite effect. It unnerved me. There was a straight forwardness to predators that I'd always appreciated. They had a goal, and they were relentless until they either killed their meal or the prey escaped.

Like last night, the prey hadn't escaped. They weren't attacking us, either. Why weren't they coming in for the kill? I knew patience was a virtue with all predators. Hunting was the epic waiting game. *An abomination of time*, my father used to call it, because hunters cannot do anything but wait. The minute you check your phone or go to the bathroom is the exact moment the quarry will cross the hunter's path. But if you don't look away, if you observe your prey, then there's that small slip of a moment where either the hunter takes down the animal, or the animal moves out of range, and all that time spent waiting becomes fruitless.

So why were these predators so different? Why were they so slow to kill? They were the opposite of relentless. They were casual killers.

"Maybe they're gone for the night," I suggested.

"These things don't act like regular animals, do they?" Mad Dog asked. He'd been coming to the same conclusion. "It's like they've already eaten and ain't hungry no more."

"It's been at least one day since they ate. I'm starving. They should be, too," I said. "So why aren't they attacking us? They have the numbers."

"Maybe they're waiting for the right moment," Mad Dog suggested.

"Maybe," I said. "I've seen lions maim a gazelle out on the savannah, and then stop attacking. They just sit down beside it and wait for the poor beast to die. Perhaps that's what they're doing. Maiming us and waiting for us to die."

I examined the bent steel of Mad Dog's traps. The light of the flames wavered in the abused angles.

"They can wait," I said. "We won't be so easily killed."

Mad Dog smiled. "Hoorah, Cody. Now, just in case those monsters come back, I'll take the first watch. I ain't sleeping after they bent my iron. You get some shut eye."

I wasn't sure anyone should be sleeping with Utahraptors lurking in the dark, but between the jarring wake-up call this morning and hiking through hard terrain all day, my body was wasted, and my legs were sore. I needed sleep.

I wanted to be ready, though, just in case, so I set my arrows beside me, within reach. I took care to ensure they were evenly spaced and not angled into the snow where the tips could rust.

Mad Dog watched me inspect the feathering and check each arrow's balance. I had my rituals.

He said, "I don't think I've ever seen anybody treat a weapon with that much respect outside of a samurai movie. It's like a spiritual thing for you."

A smile teased the side of my face.

"I didn't mean to offend."

"No, you didn't. It's just…you're not far off the mark, either. When my father taught me to hunt with a bow, he talked about energy. There was energy in the draw of the bowstring, and that energy was moved to the arrow and absorbed by the target, which was usually a deer. My father believed that you then consumed that energy by eating the deer, so in a way, the energy in the food on your table originated with the drawing back of the bowstring. He taught me to respect that energy, that dry-firing a bow was blasphemy, and to take care of the equipment implicitly. So yeah, it's always been spiritual for me."

"That is beautiful," Mad Dog said. "My Daddy didn't teach me that, but he taught me to hunt and fish the rivers of the Smoky Mountains, where I grew up. He talked about land management and harvest management as an important part of life. When we said grace, we always thanked the Lord for the hunt if we were eating venison. If he'd have known that one day I'd be hunting dinosaurs in California, he'd have lost his mind."

My ritual complete, I removed my mummy-style sleeping bag from my pack.

"Can I ask you one more question before you go to sleep? Hunter to hunter?"

I crawled into my sleeping bag. What is it about the anticipatory heat in a cold sleeping bag that feels so satisfying?

I said, "Go ahead."

"You wear a pink bracer on your arm. I don't mean to offend, and I want you to know I ain't never had a problem with them LGBTQs, but…."

"It belonged to my daughter before she was killed."

"Oh, man. I'm sorry."

I turned over to sleep. Almost immediately, my consciousness dragged me into the dark peacefulness of rest.

After a moment, Mad Dog asked, "How old was she?"

"Twelve." The word was a callous hardened in my heart.

"Bullshit. No way you're old enough to have a twelve-year-old kid."

I don't know if Mad Dog was intentionally steering the conversation away from the tragedy, but since talking about my life was easier than talking about her death, I followed his train of thought.

"She was born when I was sixteen."

"I bet that made prom awkward."

"Not at all. I didn't go. Izzy had colic. She was up crying all night. I'm real tired, Mad Dog."

"Right, right. Sorry, man."

I could feel the questions welling up in him like a volcano waiting to erupt. The night advanced into the thick winter quiet where the cold freezes sounds. His words were loud as gunfire in that quiet.

"How'd she die? My sister got the big C."

"On a hunting expedition. She hated hunting, so I bought her a complete bow and arrow set in bright pink, her favorite color. She was shot by another hunter. Died instantly. I haven't hunted since then. Not until now."

"Oh, brother, I'm sorry to hear that. It's unnatural outliving your children. But why now? Why get back in the saddle with this gig?"

"I pushed off a lot of hunts. It didn't feel right. This one is different. There's more purpose. And I feel like I'm hunting for Izzy. There was always a mama bear in her. If she'd heard that kids were killed by dinosaurs, she'd have ordered me to go after these raptors."

"Oh, hell. That's a sore story. The world's coming to an end, I tell you."

"I wouldn't disagree with you."

"Climate change, we're constantly on the brink of war, and now global pandemics. Nobody respects the old ways."

"There is no hope, no immortality. There is no good in the world. I think that's why I came out here."

**

"Wake up," Mad Dog said, shaking me. His voice sounded as gurgled as my mind.

The full moon arched high in the sky, illuminating the wilderness. Immediately, I sensed something was wrong. The fire was reduced to charcoals.

"The fire's dead. Why'd you let the fire die?" I rubbed my eyes. I'd slept so deeply, it was like coming out of frozen carbonite.

"I tried to stay awake. I think I dozed for an hour. When I woke up, the fire had died down. That's not the worst part. Those thieves snuck in here and stole all my traps back."

Indeed, the blurry images of raptor tracks and missing traps formed in my retinas, but the world was still ringed in a dark vignette. "What would raptors want with busted traps? They broke them!"

After a brief pause, he said, "That's something you'll have to figure out on your own, Cody. They got me, too."

That snapped my eyes wide open. "Wait…what?"

Mad Dog pulled back his sleeping bag to show the rip across his stomach. "I didn't even hear it happen. I just felt pressure. I opened my eyes, and that ugly cuss, Jonah, was standing over me. He raked across me with that wicked scimitar of his, and I was done. He watched me while he did it, Cody. Like he was enjoying it. I've gutted animals before, but never while they was still alive."

The cut was full of blood bright as holly berries. As it pooled under his body, the blood turned dark. Mad Dog looked like he was sitting in a puddle of red wine.

"Ohhh, God." I parsed. Finally, I managed to say, "Don't give up yet. We're not exactly gazelles, are we? Put pressure on the wound."

"Man, we're still hours out of cell tower range. I ain't living that long."

"Where did the raptors go? We'll make them pay for this."

"Ran off as soon as Jonah cut me. Maybe we are gazelles, but we ain't lions to them. He maimed me and left me to die."

He snapped the sheath of his gut hook knife and handed it to me. "Take this. You'll need it more than I will."

I studied Mad Dog's countenance. He was very pale. I didn't want to leave him.

Mad Dog coughed. "What's your daughter's name?" Mad Dog asked.

I put my hand on the back of his neck. "Isabelle."

"I'm gonna go see her in a few minutes. I'll tell her what a great daddy she has." Another cough.

My heart welled up with emotion and my eyes filled with tears. I didn't know what to say. I mean, when I went to sleep, things were dire, but I didn't expect to have this conversation when I woke up. Thankfully, Mad Dog could talk for both of us.

"Look, you got to leave me, Cody. You was right. They're after both of us. They're still after you. If you go now, they'll spend more time playing with me, which means you get a longer lead to the parking lot."

I nodded. Mad Dog and I touched foreheads, and after a moment, he pushed me away. "Go."

"Thank you," I said. "You're a good person."

"Naw, brother. I'm a Mad Dog!" He howled and yipped without energy while I grabbed my bow and arrows and my pack and ran. As soon as I left camp, a choir of metallic shrieks tore through the night.

"I got your dinner right here for ya--" Mad Dog's beleaguered war cry was cut off by the raptors.

I escaped into a terrible and gloomy forest. My foot caught on a branch, but when I looked down I saw twisted metal. It was the first of the five remaining traps, all laid out in the snow exactly where I'd run. The cruelty of their intelligence both frightened and appalled me.

This was a warning as much as it was a taunt. They knew I was alone. The last victim. I had no traps and no friends out here in the wilderness.

But I still had my bow and arrows.

CHAPTER FOUR

I fled straight toward the parking lot. No detours and no scenic routes. By my guesstimation, I could be there by noon, even if the weather turned bad.

Call my pace a forced march. Some might accuse me of being "some dumb white dude" for not running faster. *You've got raptors chasing you – run like it!* Believe me, I wanted to run as fast as my feet could carry me. I'd always been an avid runner, and once upon a time I ran in the Big Sur Marathon.

The flash of an image in my head: Kianne and Izzy in matching beanies at Mile almost-23, about thirty yards ahead of the aid station. Behind them, waves crash against the boulders along a majestic California coastline. Kianne is holding a paper Gatorade cup in her hands. I know she's exchanged the fruit punch for Red Bull and vodka because she is mischievous and always spikes my racing drinks. Izzy is six years old, and she holds above her head a sign that reads "Go Go Go Daddy!" in big, block letters. As she jumps up and down, the pom on her beanie bounces.

But unlike the roads of Big Sur, in this blighted land nobody was waiting at the aid station cheering me on. The terrain here was uncompromising and hidden beneath a layer of crisp snow. If I twisted an ankle, it'd literally be the death of me. So no, I couldn't move faster. I had to pick my foot placement carefully.

I spent the morning walking the trail. If the mountains hated me yesterday, they gnashed their teeth and cursed my presence now. I was an interloper in the wilderness, and they were fighting me. They wanted to trip me up and make me break an ankle so that the dinosaurs could eat me. That's the only explanation for just how many times rocks popped out of nowhere in the deep snow. I've been hiking or running trails like this one since I was a teen. I'm telling you, this landscape was an inhospitable kill-crush and more dangerous than any trail system I'd ever hiked.

And I know, you're going to throw out some crazy trail like Mount *Hua Shan* in China or *Caminito del Rey* in Spain. And those are dangerous, but they're more winnowing. I hiked *Caminito* while on a hunting expedition to Andalusia, and I can vouch that it's a crazy ride. The path through the Gorge of Giants is maybe three feet wide at best, with one side being vertical rock that's constantly weaving back and forth like it's trying to push you off. The other side of the path is a sheer drop. One bad step and you're another statistic along the *Caminito*. But if you have the right gear, you're no more likely to hurt yourself than you would hiking in a neighborhood park. The threats are right there in front of your face. Hidden under the cover of snow, the Perdidos trails were much, much more perilous.

The trail switched back and forth between several dark mountains, winding along the edge of a dry riverbed. I remembered being stricken when I first walked into the Perdidos by how one mountain was all picture-perfect winter scenes but the other was a scab of a mountainside. Long, black blades of leafless pine sunk askew into the somber snow. I wasn't just looking at the remnants of a forest fire, I was running through nature's cemetery, and the pines were its tombstones.

The other side of the riverbed was a Christmas card come to life. It's always striking seeing the how a wildfire can completely devastate one section of forest then miss another. Tall ponderosas were covered by chubby tufts of snow. Thick snowflakes drifted so slowly in the air, they seemed to almost levitate under St. Nick's spell. Cardinals nestled in branches ornamented with giant pinecones. I wouldn't have been surprised if Burt Ives rolled out singing "Have a Holly, Jolly Christmas."

Burt Ives or not, this passage had the cover.

I couldn't have left that scabrous trail quicker. As soon as I entered the ponderosas, the stiff cracks of claws on rocks clacked in my ears. Like bone swords unsheathing. The raptors were after me. They hadn't spent ten minutes with Mad Dog's body. They'd probably stuffed it (him) up a tree somewhere and left him to bleed to death. Now they were coming for me.

They didn't hide their hunt, either. By screaming from either side of me, the Utahraptors let me know quite clearly they were close.

Their screams chilled me, even in the middle of a winter forest. As a California kid, I've heard the stories of *La Llorona* wailing for her children. The story of the boogey woman luring little kids to a watery grave spooked me when I was a boy. As an adult, I recognize the effectiveness of the story. I don't camp near streams and rivers, and at least on one occasion that probably saved my camp from a flash flood.

It's weird how when you are young your head's filled with all these made-up fears. Is that to keep your mind off the real dangers? Heart attacks and cancer, going broke? Or is it to fill the void in happy children who don't know better than to fear things, so we tell them to be afraid of the river and the dark woods?

Unless you're an avid outdoorsman, I'll tell you another thing to fear: animal noise. I'm not talking woodpeckers and chipmunks. I'm talking top-of-the-food-chain animal noise. Big predators like tigers and bears hunt in silence. They don't announce their presence until they're on top of you and it's too late. It's the golden rule of natural predation. Keep quiet or spook your prey.

These raptors were happy to announce their position to me. It meant either they were overconfident in the kill or that they didn't care whether or not they caught me. Like everything else I'd learned about them, their confidence was so unnatural, it filled me with dread. It's been estimated that most predators are successful hunters less than ten percent of the time. That's why they're so cautious and careful. These raptors, though. If the natural rules of predation didn't apply to raptors, then they were like no other creatures on Earth, and I had no idea how to escape them.

That fear in the back of my head convinced me to pick up my tempo from a forced march to a light jog. I said a quick prayer that I wouldn't pull a tendon and that my energy wouldn't give out. Fast-paced walking along a sidewalk with temperatures in the sixties was the epitome of ease, and I can imagine in many places what I'd done that morning was an off-day workout. But compounded by stress, snow, and altitude trekking, my off-day workout had transformed into a crushing workout. And it was only getting tougher.

I had to keep my eyes constantly shifting from about five feet in front of me to right under my boots. It took a couple of minutes to acclimate to the back and forth, but once I did, I had no problem discovering potential ankle-twisters and toe-stubbers. As a rule, I kept a wide birth from the slightest rises and dips of snow.

My running partners picked up their pace, too.

They want to run me to death, I thought. *That's alright. The joke's on them. I qualified for the Boston Marathon. I can run all day if they want.*

If they wanted. I wasn't sure. At any moment, they could decide they were tired of the game.

And I wasn't so sure I could run all day.

I hit a rock with the back of my foot. Left some hand skin on the ground, but I kept my forward momentum. My heart rate spiked. Was this it?

The raptors were closer. Still two or three times their length away from me.

Once more, my many years studying predator/prey behavior kicked in. If I slowed down even a little, the Utahraptors would assume I was injured and take me down. If I picked up speed, so would they, but then I'd have to commit to that speed. So I compromised with the light jog. It was fast enough to show my health, but slow enough that I could maintain my pace.

Occasionally, one of the raptors would give that electric banshee howl that made me jump. Sometimes it was farther away, but sometimes it was much closer. When it was much closer, I felt that ice-cold finger running up my back.

They're trying to spook you into running faster, I thought. Well, it was spooky. It was scary as hell, and I'd hunted man-eating lions. I was surrounded by ugly mountains and a gray-lidded sky, the color of a cast iron pot before it's seasoned. The clouds and the mountains were pressing down on me. Even in the early morning, the world seemed dark and lonely and burdensome. When the path forced me to return to the forest fire graveyard, everything became that much more foreboding.

I took a deep breath and exhaled my fear. *Keep your pace.*

And then I laughed. It just came out of me, like a warm soda's burp. My mind had started wandering again. I had this silly thought. *'Cause running from monsters is good exercise, right?* So I wondered, *should I check my splits? Was I having a good mile?*

You think of the weirdest things running for your life.

Occasionally, I'd catch one of the Utahraptors out of the corner of my eye. Running between the trees. Sticking to the shadows. Bodies rippling with muscle.

I couldn't think about them. If I did, I might start to run quicker, and that'd be the nail in my coffin.

To pass the time, I reminded myself why I was there in the first place.

Early January in southern California is a dull, winterless onslaught of endless sunrises and sunsets. Some people worship it, but to me one day blends into the next. Perfect temperature, little wind, no rain. Living like that, the mind becomes a drought itself, craving green. Suicides increase. Hypertension goes up. Did you know that some restaurants in LA paint green to combat the psychological loss of the rainless eternity? Well, more like paint it green because people are attracted to the greenscapes. They crave the effect of water on the land, its magic-like restorative properties. Even when they cannot see it, they yearn for it. That's why Californians love the ocean.

My home was full of all the things I loved, and since the death of my wife and daughter it was completely, utterly empty because it was full of all the things I loved. I sat on the sofa where my daughter and I played video games. I ate at the table where I helped her finish math homework. The table itself was oak. Sturdy. Long-lasting. The kind of table that you pass down for generations. But without my daughter, the table had become a memory that was getting weaker with every month, like a cavity in my brain.

At my wife's funeral, people told me Kianne would live on in my daughter. "She will live in your hearts and her memory will keep her alive." And then at Izzy's funeral, they said the same thing. Izzy would live in my heart. That's bullshit. After everyone left and I was alone in my house, I wept and clung to the memories of my wife and daughter, and the harder I held on to them, the more they seemed to escape. I worried there would come a day when I wouldn't have any memories left. My wife and my daughter would fade into this gray, colorless thing that wasn't really a memory but more like how a photo can become a memory if you look at it day after day after day. It isn't a memory. It's a photo that you've turned into the memory. You don't remember what was happening outside the photo, or what it smelled like or whether it was cold or hot that day.

If my memories faded, what would become of them, and what would become of me?

The doctor had called. It was time for our office check-ups. Being a widower and a single parent, I'd scheduled both my appointment and Izzy's for the same day. I had to explain that my daughter was dead and wouldn't be at the appointment. This was not the first or the ninth time I'd had to do this. There were dentists, eye doctors, parks and rec departments, schools, teachers, phone companies.... My life was a cycle of explanations and unsubscribes for people no longer tethered to our planet. And it wasn't constant, not the way most people think of it. Sure, in the first days and weeks it was endless, but then it settled into a strange cycle. Just as I would be feeling better, I would get a phone call or an e-mail. I'd be thrust back into the loneliness and the sadness.

I was in the waiting room of my doctor's office, filling out forms on the clipboard so that I could get my annual checkup. Name, social security number, past medical history. Allergies. Emergency Contact Information. I saw that blank line, and it was like a blank line into my heart. The cycle of pain was renewed again.

Who could I put down? My parents were dead. My wife was deceased. I'd recently buried my daughter. I had no emergency contact. I had nobody to go to, and I'd preferred it that way. I'd avoided friends, conversations, get-togethers. I changed my work schedule to telework. When people asked to have me over or get together online or go hunting or even "Hell, let's just go hiking, Cody!", I gave an excuse about needing to take care of funeral arrangements, but the truth is that I was just extricating myself from that world.

I don't know where I was going or why I was leaving, but slowly I was receding into the dark. Maybe I hoped I would become a faded memory even to myself, and then I'd just be gone. That would be better than what was left of my life.

I didn't escape into the typical vices. I didn't drink or do drugs. But I'd be lying if I didn't admit that I'd had suicidal thoughts. Go ahead and judge me on that, but screw you. All my family was dead. Stolen from me.

To take from my family's parlance, my energy was wasted. There was no point to it. I was a bowstring being pulled back and dry-fired over and over without an arrow ever touching the string. And like a bow, I knew I'd break. I could feel the stress in my arch. My limbs were cracking. My cams were chinking. If I didn't do something, I'd shatter into a hundred pieces.

I made an appointment to see the doctor. And sitting in the stiff black sofa, pen in hand, I broke down. I couldn't stop crying. I rubbed the tears from my eyes, and I tried to hide my shame. I was so embarrassed. People stared. I walked to the counter, clipboard in hand and picked a tissue from the box.

In the same tone a person might use when they pull over to check on a motor vehiclist with a flat tire but they don't know how to change a flat tire or want to stop, the woman at the counter asked me, "Are you okay?"

"No, not really," I said.

"Maybe you should…" and she let her words trail into nothing. The phone rang and she picked it up, happy to not have to deal with human emotions. I blew my nose and sat back down and stared at that blank line. The elderly couple sitting across from me jumped out of their seats when the nurse called their name. They couldn't leave my area fast enough.

My phone buzzed in my jeans pocket. I ignored it because I assumed it was another random company saying that Izzy's subscription needed to be renewed. Or maybe it was Disney wanting to talk to me about that great family vacation they were always trying to sell me. But I couldn't ignore it. What is it about ringing phones that they have to be answered?

I recognized the text as belonging to a buddy of mine who was now a clerk for Sheriff Castillo. I knew I needed a change, and if hunting is what had sent me spiraling into this hell, maybe it would redeem me, too. Or kill me. Death by dinosaur, right?

CHAPTER FIVE

I couldn't keep thinking like that. I focused on the parking lot instead and what I would do once I got there. "Parking lot" was a bit of an exaggeration. Our cars sat in an open field covered in snow. Two old logs, hidden in the snow now, acted as pylons. At the far side of the field a frame of cut timber marked the trail entrance. This was a county trail, not a state or Federal trail. It was poorly sustained. The path winded a twenty-mile loop along a riverbed. What once was the Calavera River (and now was little more than an indentation in the ground) received its name because, according to local legend, early Spanish settlers found an abandoned roundhouse here. The roundhouse was full of skulls.

When the county park was created, the beautiful Calavera showed off tall, majestic pine trees. Stately Coulters and Ponderosas, narrow Sugar Pines, and purple-barked Western Pines grew here. The trail was also great for bird watching, and not just goldfinches and warblers, but also condors and eagles. Since the river dried up and the fires burned through, there was little fascination with this scarred wilderness.

History and geography aside, I needed a plan for the parking lot. The raptors would come at me fast. My Silverado was the third car in. Jan drove a Cherokee, Mad Dog an F-150.

Third car in.

Keys? I padded my pants. Check.

The driver's side door was on the far side. I'd have to run alongside the cars and come around the end of the Silverado to open the door. Thank God the truck had a remote start. I'd never been so thankful for it. Car engines roaring to life frighten even the largest animals. A dinosaur, which had never heard an engine before (fingers crossed) would scare easily once I hit the engine start button. If that wasn't enough, there was that panic button. My life would be saved by a state-of-the-art key fob. That made me chuckle.

I kept running.

I imagined myself entering the parking lot. I'd throw my pack in the truck bed as well as the bow and arrows. I wished I could be kinder to my instruments of war.

I remember something my father used to say. *These are not phones that you replace every two years. If you take care of your bow and arrows, they will serve your family for generations.*

Dad's advice rang empty on me. There was no next generation. But I still felt a familial duty to protect them. At the same time, I didn't want to die. Despite my suicidal thoughts, I was still fully loaded with a sense of self-preservation. I may have wanted to kill myself, but I wasn't going to allow a raptor to kill me.

Priorities. I had no family to pass on the hunting traditions. I'd been an only child, and I had no nieces or nephews. So, toss the bow and arrows in the back of the truck.

A fallen tree laid across the trail. I recognized the scale-armor latticework of the oak's bark. I was getting close. I'd been jogging for two hours, and the raptors hadn't claimed my life yet.

But then a Utahraptor stood up from behind the log. It was the monster with the half-burned face. Jonah.

Dinosaurs don't get scars like humans because their bodies are covered in scales and feathers instead of flesh. So, I agreed with Jan's original assessment of Jonah – half his face was melted off. He looked kind of like Jonah Hex, or Two-Face from Batman comics. However, while one eye seemed to bulge out of his face, I knew that in reality it was a missing face that caused the bulging, not an enlarging of the eye.

His burns were a series of twisted vertices where chunks of flesh were ripped from his face. In their place, each scar was a pale, almost luminescent patchwork outlined in thin, black scales.

A human with that kind of facial damage might be saddened by other people's staring and judgements. But Jonah's eyes showed no emotion. He didn't give a damn what you thought of his burn, and I doubted the other raptors cared, either. They only cared about the hunt.

So did I.

The ugly dinosaur hissed. The sibilant sound coming from his mouth was a busted pipe when the air forces high-pitched and strong through a thin crack. A jump scare of fright exploded from deep inside me. Keep in mind, I'm all alone in the middle of the wilderness, and something that looks like a cross between a raptor and the devil has jumped out from behind a tree. I turned and ran back the way I came, hating my luck.

This was it. They were coming for me. I suspected the two raptors would lunge at me from either side. When they appeared in the corner of my eyes, I jerked behind a tree. The raptors nearly crashed into each other. They were so close I could smell their rank breath. If I wanted to, I could reach out and grab one of their tails and wag it like a dog's. Not that I had any desire to do that. Each raptor was as tall as a black bear and as long as a mountain lion.

The difference between raptors and the bears that I'd hunted is that bears didn't have stamina like this. I doubted mountain lions did, either.

I zig-zagged into the dead trees, hoping that the higher elevation would throw them off.

Let me skip to the bad part: it didn't work. But if anything was saving me, it was their lack of urgency. For some unknown reason, they still weren't ready to kill me yet. The Tres Amigos from hell chased me nonchalantly. I knew I couldn't keep this tempo going uphill, so I lowered my elevation and ran alongside the dry Calavera River. While I ran, I tried to think of another way back to the parking lot. Stopping to grab a map would be fatal. Even if the raptors didn't catch me and kill me during that pause, I'd have to study the damn thing while running. That was asking for disaster. Remember, those Perdidos were still trying to make me lose my footing and stumble with every step. Even on a clear trail, little clastic rocks always seemed to find their way under my feet. And there were only two kinds of rocks on this trail: slippery or jagged.

Besides, the map was in my backpack side pocket. I couldn't reach it without stopping.

Eventually I would have to rest. I couldn't run forever. I was at the mercy of my own biology. Lungs or legs, one of them would give out. Now that the raptors had returned to their lazy chase, I reduced my speed to a jog. I was wary of their reaction, but they didn't attack, so they must have perceived me as still relatively healthy. Or they had worse plans in mind. At this point, I couldn't tell.

In my mind, I tried to imagine the map as I remembered it. The leaflet was old, and it didn't cover much mileage, but there was a second trail leading back to the parking lot. Getting to it meant climbing Brideshead Mountain and crossing the second trail on the other side of the mountain.

Did I have the energy to get that far, though? I was seriously starting to doubt myself, physically. I was bone-tired. If I was running a marathon, there'd be cups of water and electrolytes and protein snacks at every mile. Even most ultramarathons offered refreshments every five to ten miles. But not here. And to add insult to injury, I wasn't in marathon shape. Yet I'd been jogging all morning.

And hiking all the day before.

And carrying a deer the day before that.

I won't lie. The odds didn't look good.

I kept moving.

Going up the mountain slowed me down, and this time my reduced speed excited the raptors. They saw that I was getting tired and quickened their pace. Was this the end? Had my uphill climb doomed me? No longer on the edges of my peripheral, the dinosaurs shrieked from closer and closer distances.

Okay, you're driving me. But where? And why? You can kill me now if you wanted.

I tampered my fear reaction, which told me to sprint. It was a really powerful instinct trying to kick in, but it was also exactly what would get me killed. I couldn't sprint for more than ten or twenty yards uphill before I'd overdo it and have to stop completely, and then they'd have me. So I pushed the fear down.

I self-assessed. Throat dry, lungs burning. Most people think that running in the cold is easy as hunting a drunk squirrel. Sure, when it's "cooler," running can be easier on your whole body. But in freezing weather what happens is your body is taking all that cold, dry air into your lungs, and the air dehydrates you quickly. It is the opposite effect of what you'd think because you're losing water like you're running through Death Valley. So even though I was surrounded by frozen water everywhere, my body was aching for hydration. "Water, water everywhere and not a drop to drink!"

I gulped from my reservoir and continued the self-check.

No chafing, thank God. I've seen elite runners taken out in the middle of competition by chafing. My left knee was beginning to complain like a middle child, too. It was an old injury that called out to me whenever I overused it, and while I'd been lucky and not slipped on a rock, the mountains were punishing my joints. Mentally, I considered myself in good shape. I wasn't depressed; I believed I could still escape, though I knew that every minute spent trail running reduced my chances of survival.

I discovered an animal trail in between *manzanitas* and jogged it for a mile before the trail turned away from Brideshead. I cut through the blackened, cadaverous trees. By this point, my feet were noticeably dragging. At first, only one out of every 100 steps skidded across the rocks and snow. Always my left foot. But then it was one out of every fifty and then one out of every twenty, and by the time I hit the animal trail, my boots sounded like a tambourine slapping against the alluvium and ice. Very dangerous. I had to concentrate on lifting my boots, but they were *so heavy*.

I must have zoned out concentrating so hard on lifting my feet with what little energy I had left. Not long after, I realized I was alone. I couldn't see or hear the raptors anymore. *What are they up to?* I wondered. What new plan do they have for me?

I worried that I wasn't hearing them over all the noise I was making, so I put extra effort into my stride, swallowed my breath, and tuned my ears to the forest. I didn't hear the devils anymore.

I didn't trust these dinosaurs, so I didn't abandon my stride. They could be running up ahead of me again, or perhaps they figured out that I was crossing Brideshead and were taking an alternative route. I'd like to think they gave up the chase. With predators, that happened. They weren't hungry (I felt a slight pang in my heart for Mad Dog and Jan). There was no benefit to a prolonged, calorie-wasting hunt.

These raptors didn't feel like those kinds of predators, though.

Ultimately, I dared to slow my pace to a walk. I ran out of steam and couldn't maintain that tempo. I needed a break. I took it while approaching the col. The col is the low point of a ridge or saddle between two peaks, in this case the low point between Brideshead and Kill Devil Mountain.

I created my own switchbacks, semi-confident that the raptors were no longer chasing me. But the problem with trailblazing is that you are forging your own trails. The soles of my feet became a magnet to every rock and pinecone in the forest. One time, I rolled on a snow-covered pinecone. I splayed around like a windmill. Luckily, I regained my footing before dropping my tailbone on a jagged granite tooth.

My boots, waterproof as they were, were not made for sloshing through snowbanks. Cold wetness wrapped around my feet. First I felt it on the boot, then in my wool socks. I got that sinking feeling I was also feeling cold water on my skin. Damn, I hoped not. Maybe that was just the paranoia of frostbite.

At the top of the col, my body gave out. I stood there in the snow and ice, leaning over, huffing and panting. I swallowed some water from my Camelbak. Once my breath and my pulse had slowed, I scanned the mountains around me.

Blurry clouds pushed from the west, dropping snow that erased the mountain range behind it. That snow would reach Brideshead by nightfall. Perhaps the raptors disappeared to find a warm place to ride out the storm.

I searched the trails behind me for any signs of raptors in the hellscape of dead trees.

Wind howled and tree branches rattled, but there was no sign of life except my own. I dropped my pack, drank plentifully from my

Camelbak, then shoveled GORP (Good Ole Raisins and Peanuts) into my mouth. Rehydrated and re-fueled, I checked once more for raptors. One long minute later (it felt more like five), I decided the raptors had left me.

Unfortunately, the snowstorm was coming in faster than I'd assumed. Certainly, this was the reason the raptors gave up the chase. That storm saved my life. The way my feet were dragging, I couldn't have maintained my pace for much longer before falling over in exhaustion. But like always with nature, what was a savior was also a curse. Night would be much colder, and I'd run away from camp without packing my sleeping bag.

I tried to get a signal, but still no bars.

The thermometer on my backpack read subzero temperatures. Not below freezing. Not 10 degrees. Negative 7 degrees.

I finally checked my map. I was glad I had the foresight to laminate it before I joined the expedition.

Always make sure you have a good map, I remembered telling Izzy. *Don't trust that your GPS will work everywhere.*

The trail dropped five hundred feet from the col to the valley below. Then, it was another eight miles to the parking lot. God, I wanted to push myself and run to the parking lot. I would feel so much safer sleeping in my truck.

I had to face reality, though. Even if I was fit and rested, there was no way I could outrun the storm to the Silverado. My guesstimation, I'd still be two or three miles out when the storm hit. The storm looked nasty. I saw myself covered in ice, dying of hypothermia and still out of eyesight of the parking lot.

So be it. One more night on the trail. But I needed a place to pitch my tent.

Fortunately, the map had my answer. An old California Scouts Wilderness Survival camp. I doubted the camp kept any equipment or sleeping bags, but it would have sheltered locations to camp.

I descended the col, following a draw down to the valley floor. I elected to stay on the top edge of the draw, despite the danger, because my visual acuity was much better from that angle. I could see to the north and south while holding the high ground. It wasn't lost on me that I was behaving like a prey animal. That was fine. I'd been prey before.

Still, tread carefully, right? Falling was always more likely to happen descending rather than ascending. Fifty feet from the top of the col, my left leg swiped out like I'd walked across wet glass. My body followed, and the next thing I knew, I was sliding down the edge of the mountain. A wave of snowdrift followed me as I tumbled.

An icepick could be used to glissade to a stop. I cursed myself for not bringing it. My second thought was to use my arrows, but even the sturdiest-constructed arrows would snap trying to hold my weight, so I couldn't stab them in the snow like a bad ass and hope for the best. Before my third thought, the snow swirled me around. My snowdrift had evolved into a sort-of avalanche. Snow surged behind me and lifted me up. I looked over my shoulder. Several black-topped boulders jutted out of the snow like molars. There was also a small pine tree. Beyond the rocks and tree was a fifty-foot drop-off. The trees at the bottom looked downright diminutive by comparison.

Don't hit the rock. Don't hit the rock.

I hit the rock, grunted, and became airborne. I flew with all the grace of a drunk goose. But instead of going over the ledge, I landed in a thorny bush that ripped my jacket and pants, but thank God it stopped my fall.

I groaned. I'd hit the rock with the back of my thigh. My hamstring was sore as hell, but I could walk on it. I had ibuprofen in my first aid kit. My bigger problem was that my clothes were completely soaked with freezing water. Snow had been shoved in places where nothing should be shoved, and now my body was warming it all up. Left unchecked, I'd be dealing with hypothermia and frostbite.

I removed all clothes that weren't Gore-Tex hiking boots and limped naked the rest of the way to the valley floor. I kept thinking of Bigfoot as I made my way down the draw. If somebody happened to be out in this remote area, would they think my bare butt was Sasquatch?

Nah. I wasn't that tall.

Still, it was a fun distraction to think about being misidentified as Bigfoot. I needed some positive thoughts. All alone in a wilderness that hates you is not a place where you want to get the blues. What was it I'd always heard? You can go three minutes without air, three days without water, and three weeks without food, but not three seconds without positive mental attitude? Corny, sure, but true.

So, Bigfoot stomped his bare-naked bod through the bone-shivering winter, mooning any creature that looked for him.

By the time I reached the valley floor, my body was dry enough that I could throw thermals over my skin. Thank God for thermal underwear. They were a lifesaver.

When I arrived at the wilderness camp, I dropped my backpack and shouted out in triumph. The first thing I shouted wasn't really a word, more an emotional expression. But my second showed my maturity in the face of adversity.

"EAT MY ASS, YOU STUPID RAPTORS!!!"

So much had happened to me that day. It felt like a relief to have reached the encampment. Waves of raw energy and joy rippled from me. I couldn't celebrate for very long, though. I needed a fire and a shelter.

The camp had plenty of logs to sleep under, and right then I was really tempted to crawl under a log and be done for the day, but if I was being honest (and I come from a long line of trustworthy and honest people), those logs gave next to no protection against Utahraptors. And then there was the whole hypothermia/frostbite thing.

The more I thought about it, I could set up my tent, but it'd be a homing beacon to the raptors. And this was only one night. Last night in the woods. I could survive better outside of a tent than in one if I had the right hiding place.

As I was searching for the perfect log to crawl under, I found something spectacular. The Taj Mahal of wilderness camps. The camp's grand site, clearly built to impress young scouts with the possibilities of wilderness survival. The hut was narrow and long and constructed from thick branches and tree trunks. It was more of a trench than a hut. I don't think it cleared three feet over the snow. Pine branches lay on top of the trench for insulation. I could have cried, I was so happy.

As for configuration, the hut lay off to the side and out of the way. I almost missed it, even though it opened to the valley floor.

This would do perfectly.

CHAPTER SIX

Despite my joy, I was so tired. My legs were lead. They thudded with each step in the snow. But I couldn't sleep before I'd prepped my shelter. I hadn't configured anything like this in a long time. Usually there was some kind of modern lodging (hotel, resort, or tent) where I hunted. It took me back to my Scouting days, before I ever met Kianne and long before Izzy was born.

My mind was fuzzy from running all day. A weight at the back of my head warned me to lie down or be forced to lie down. I couldn't.

First, I needed to check for the five Ws: widowmakers, water, wigglies, weather, and wood. Tucked into pine-covered timberland with a storm inbound, I wasn't worried about water or wood. Wind and weather were the main concerns. The storm would cross the hut perpendicular to its design, which meant it would probably cause very little damage. The danger was in its entrance. Even with the storm coming from its direction, some wind would flow into the trench. I needed a door and insulation if I was to survive the night.

Fortunately, early winter storms had knocked down enough tree branches that I didn't need to hack many with the camp axe. If I'd needed to cut more than a handful, I think I would've given up. The wood I wanted was at least a half inch in diameter, but preferably over an inch, and at least three to four feet long. While I collected the branches, I checked for "widowmakers," large, overhanging branches that could injure if they fell on my head. As suspected, the California Scouts kept the shelter area clear of dangerous branches. I stacked several, broken-end up, against the sides of the shelter so that the snow would drain down.

The branches were better than nothing, but as insulation goes, they were pretty shoddy, so I stuffed pine into the deepest part of the trench.

Hands shaking, I cut apart my tent's camouflage rain fly and tied it to two branches using extra paracord. *Always Bring Paracord!* I warned Izzy when we would go camping. The adage saved my bacon that night.

Shelter complete, it was time to prepare in case the raptors returned. I whittled off the ends of unused branches. I wished I had my family's bowie knife, but I left it at home, which was too bad. There were some interesting legends about the Morris family hunting knife. I used my pocketknife, a Petzl with a strong blade. Much smaller than Mad Dog's gut hook, the Petzl was almost useless against a raptor, but one of the mantras of wilderness survival is to find the purpose in everything, and the Petzl was perfect for whittling. I buried the sticks straight up and down in the snow around the shelter. I'd need to dig them up before I left. And I planned on leaving as soon as the storm eased up.

After setting up the sticks, I created a dinosaur early warning system, twenty yards out from the shelter. Using more paracord, I tied together not just my cup and pot, but anything I could find in my pack, anything that was metallic or would make a noise if it knocked something, say an attacking Utahraptor. That included my mirror, prismatic compass, safety pins, the multi-tool scissors that separated in the middle, a couple of extra carabiners, and even one of my two pairs of binoculars. I was pretty much throwing all this away, but underestimating the amount of junk I needed to invest in my alarm might risk my being killed.

I would set up one cord, then stick my hands in my armpits for a few minutes to warm them up. In this way, I worked my way around the perimeter of the shelter. When it was done, I wanted to stop and congratulate myself, but I was limited on time and energy, and I had more work to do.

The first idea was to create a classic deadfall, but there wasn't a rock big enough to kill a full-sized Utahraptor, and my hands and cheeks were getting so cold they felt like rock slabs on my skin. I didn't want to risk frostbite or hypothermia, so I couldn't do anything fancy. All I wanted to do was create a menace. So I set up what was left of my tent away from the shelters. I took the old standout – hanging wire, and I made a giant loop. I twisted the other end around a stick sandwiched between two spry pines. At least one raptor would get its foot caught in the wire. They would definitely break the stick and escape – I wasn't trying to capture the monster – but that wire would slice deeper and deeper into the raptor's leg. Let's see it run with that thing carving it up like a Christmas turkey!

The trench butted against a stout Ponderosa. I considered creating an escape route from the shelter by tying rope to a branch high up in the pine. If the worst happened, I could climb up the rope and out of the shelter.

The plan didn't feel right. If the dinosaurs came for me that night, my best bet was to burrow just as deep in the trench as possible, deep like a tick in a dog's hide, then shoot at the dinos with my bow and arrows. If that failed, it was the gut hook knife.

I reeeeeeally hoped it wouldn't come down to the gut hook.

***

The wind whipped up, and the dark snowstorm blurred the valley behind me. Half an hour ago I could see all the way to the draw I came down, but once again the world was being erased around me.

Time for my snughole. With any luck, I'd get a good night's sleep and be back in town by mid-morning.

Yeah, I laughed at myself, too.

I crawled into the shelter. Inside, I cut the rest of my tent into strips and tucked the ribbons between the branches. My wet jacket, socks, and clothes were also tucked in the branches so that they could dry out.

My toes were bright red, not black, so no frostbite. Afforded this relief, I spent the next ten minutes trying to create a spark from my magnesium fire starter kit. This task alone was as Herculean as running all day from raptors. It was like I was trying to replace all the little gears in a Roomba and not lose any of the screws. My numb fingers struggled with the simplest task of forcing a spark. Eventually, I generated an ember, which I blew into my tinder and birthed a small fire. I didn't need a big one. The shelter was built to trap in heat. Narrow gaps in the top of the shelter acted as a chimney.

I gulped more water, then laid out my broadpoint arrows, saying my prayer. Prayer calmed and refocused me, especially when it was complemented by the fire. My bow and arrows, I placed beside me. On my right lay the compound bow. On the other side lay the arrows. I inspected them for cracks or bends. One nock needed to be replaced. The little U-shaped crevice where the arrow sits into the bowstring was bent. Using pliers and a bit of glue, I replaced the nock.

Finally, I was ready for bed. With the snowstorm pounding against the shelter, I devoured a couple of Clif Bars. The flood of carbs and calories overloaded my weary body. I succumbed to the exhaustion almost immediately, sleeping like a mummy with my hands folded into my armpits.

Funny as it sounds, it was silence that woke me. After hours of driving winds and snow slamming against the shelter, everything suddenly went silent, and that was enough to startle me into consciousness. The storm had pushed through. I checked my watch. It was two in the morning.

Time to go home.

The shelter was completely dark. My small fire had drained its fuel hours ago. I was alone with my body and frosted exhalations. They were little apparitions of a life and heat that once was.

My body protested. An ugly, purple bruise on my hip protested the slightest movement. Along with overworked muscles, they hurled insults via my central nervous system. Well, they'd just have to go on hating me. When I was back in the Chevy with the engine running and tires taking me away from this nightmare, then I'd listen to them. Until then, I'd silence my pain receptors with ibuprofen.

I slid the button to turn on my headlamp. In the lamplight, scraps of tent material bulged inward with the weight of snow upon them. I crawled forward, mindful of my broadpoints. I pushed against the front door, but it didn't budge.

I pulled back the rain fly. A fat belly of snow filled the space where the opening should be.

"Son of a," I muttered. I pawed at the snow with my gloved hands and dumped the removed snow to my side.

Then I thought I heard something. I stopped and listened, especially for the clanging of metal.

Nothing.

I dug some more. The noise came again. A scratching sound. I was sure of it this time. Something was digging on the other side of the snow. It made no sense that any animal or dinosaur would be out in this weather. There was no chance that it was a person, but then again, what else could it be?

Welcome to your first auditory hallucination, I thought.

I was about to say something when a wolf howled far in the distance. The wolf's sound made me pause. My neck hairs stood on end. I waited for a second wolf to howl back, perhaps from a few feet away.

No response.

The wolf moon must be out, I thought. Again, I heard the digging. It wasn't small, like a mouse. It sure sounded like a human hand.

"Hello?" I called out into the silent void of the wilderness.

A raptor wailed loud and strong on the other side of the snow. I covered my ears, it was so loud!

I jumped back. This was it. I must have slept too long, or they came before the storm ended. Mother Nature had betrayed me. The snow fell too deep for my warning system to work right. I'd miscalculated, and my miscalculation might cost me my life.

I shuffled quickly to the back of the shelter and grabbed my compound bow. I picked up a broadpoint arrow, but couldn't nock it yet. I fumbled with my finger release 'cause I'd slept with my hands in wool gloves and I was scared clumsy. I yanked off the gloves and put the purple piece of metal in my right hand. The device was curved to fit the form of my fingers, and allowed me to release the arrow without stripping the skin.

My wide eyes watched the tunnel entrance. I couldn't see shit. I turned on my headlamp. There was no point trying to hide anymore.

Fragile flakes drifted from the belly of snow on the far end of the shelter. I listened to a raptor scraping wildly at the snowbank. Soon, that predator would be in here with me. I took a deep breath and exhaled slowly to steady my nerves. I placed the arrow into its rest and drew back on the string. I felt the energy in the bow as its limbs curled backward.

Then the snow bulged inward and back, clumping to the sides. Fresh chilled air swept into my shelter.

To my pink arm brace, I whispered, "I always loved you, Isabelle."

My warm breath phantomized in the frigid air. Was this what was meant by giving up the ghost?

Outside, the raptors screamed. I located them by their cries. Two had flanked either side of the trench while the third waited at the front entrance. My decision to not create an escape route paid off. If I'd scurried up the tree, the raptors would've nabbed me for sure.

The two raptors on the side ran to the front, screaming like the devil. Their vocalizations were so horrible, they robbed me of any warmth. I shuddered uncontrollably.

More high-pitched roars charged with electricity. What the hell was going on up there?

The screaming was cut short, and then the opening broke apart. Snow shot inward everywhere. This was finally it. I didn't need to sight my bow at this point, but I singled out the center of the tunnel with my bow's sighting pin. Shadows appeared and disappeared.

A large beast ran at me, all noise and frenzy. I released the arrow. Tension went out of my body, like a popped balloon. Kinetic energy flew past my cheeks, past the beast, and somehow struck the raptor chasing it. At this range, the arrow went straight through the raptor's hand. The raptor recoiled and disappeared into the night.

I would've cheered at that moment. If I don't love me, who will, right? But I couldn't.

A blood-soaked eye stared back at me through my sighting pins.

A wolf stood over me. It was the largest of its kind I'd ever seen. He barely fit in the trench. Steam rose from his back, giving him the appearance that he was on fire. His fur was covered in blood. The whole image was more than enough to suck the moment out of me. Instead of firing another arrow, I gaped at the magnificent horror.

He was gray except for black and white streaks highlighting his face. Blood dripped from his mouth. The giant wolf looked down upon me as if summing me up. I tell you, he was close enough to bite my head off. I smelled dead animals on his breath. Then as quickly as he entered, the beast spun about and ran outside barking. The raptors yelled angrily at the new challenger.

What?

Seriously. What??

I needed a second to come to my senses. Seeing opportunity, I shook myself from my gawking and grabbed an arrow and crawled out of there. When I exited the trench, I discovered that the snow was three feet deep everywhere. My knees disappeared into the banks. My early warning system was submerged in white mounds.

Arcs of blood crisscrossed around the shelter. At least one of the raptors was bleeding (*good!*), but they were now cornering the wolf.

Something primal took a hold of me. I lined up a raptor in my sight. The dinosaur paused to stare down the wolf. I fired at its back. Unfortunately, the wolf lunged, and the raptor jumped out of the way as I released the arrow. The shaft flashed in the night and stabbed a tree, exploding in the bark.

The raptors and the wolf looked back at me. I was a small man surrounded by giant monsters. That was a real sphincter-puckering moment.

"Just ignore me?"

Stupid fool - I hadn't grabbed a second arrow! The wolf chomped down hard on the hand of the raptor I'd missed. The Utahraptor shrieked. It jumped back hard enough to avoid the full clamp of the wolf's jaws.

The raptors hissed at me and retreated. The wolf limped back into the forest and disappeared into the darkness.

I stood alone in the snow, heaving, adrenaline surging. I took in the visualization of the battlefield around me: blood, mud, and snow. Did that really just happen? I returned to the trench and looked at the opening, trying to make sense of my previous minute of life. The cold and naked opening offered no answers.

A moment later, the horned shadow of the wolf's head appeared in the entrance, silhouetted against the snow. His two ears stuck out on either side. Crenels of a crown worn by the conquerors of a land that knew no humans. One ear was horribly mangled, like somebody had taken a giant hole punch to it.

The wolf lowered his head as he walked inside and joined me in the back of the trench.

I pushed my arrows out of the way as his massive form filled the narrow survival enclosure. The wolf froze for a moment, then laid down on all fours and licked his crimson-colored paws.

PART TWO: WOLVES OF PANGAEA

It was the masterful and incommunicable wisdom of eternity laughing at the futility of life and the effort of life. It was the Wild, the savage, frozen-hearted Northland Wild.
— Jack London, <u>White Fang</u>

I against my brothers. My brothers and I against my cousins. My brothers, my cousins, and I against the world.
-Pashtun proverb

CHAPTER ONE

The lone wolf puppy lay alone and destitute on a ledge so narrow his hind legs dangled off the side. He was big for his age, which was four months, but he didn't know that. Nor did he know the name of the mountain, New Profanity. If he'd been told the mountain's name or its history, he might have simply jumped off the ledge and ended his temporary existence right then and there. But the puppy knew only what his mother and the pack had taught him. That information did not include the names of mountains.

He opened his mouth. Bright white teeth, young teeth, shined in the daylight. The puppy wanted to whine but dared not. He studied the precipice rising above him.

His sides hurt from falling down the side of the mountain, and his stomach ached for food. He was barely old enough to eat on his own, much less hunt for his own sustenance, but again, the lone wolf did not know that. He was ignorant.

Slowly, he pulled himself along the ledge, fumbling over rocks. Once, he almost fell because his legs were so tired that they would not hold him up. He dragged his hindquarters back up onto the ledge and crawled the rest of the way onto the mountain proper.

Blood covered the rocks before him. His den reeked of slaughter. His older sister lay in a pool of blood that had leaked from her body and turned sticky. Two vultures tugged at her mutilated corpse.

The puppy spotted his mother. He ran to her and nuzzled her face, hoping for some kindness, but she did not respond. Her fur was stained with her own blood. The young wolf knew this meant he needed to run away immediately, but he didn't want to run. He cried out for his mother, a pitiful yet endearing yip of a howl.

Nature is not kind, though. His howl drew the attention of one of the vultures. It hopped toward him, spittle and blood dripping from its black beak.

The wolf saw the vulture's ugly face reflected in his mother's dead pupils. He jumped just in time as the vulture jabbed at him. The puppy ran away. He loped down the mountainside. Along the way, he caught the scent of his father and his brothers. Smelling their blood and offal, he cautiously approached their bodies.

Already, their ribs had been picked clean. He hesitated at his father's face. Both eyes were missing from his otherwise perfect head. The pup sniffed his father's nose. The head rolled around, scaring him. The puppy ran behind a black pine and hid. His body juddered with fear. He panted until he felt better, then looked back out at the corpse. He choked down his fear and walked back to his father's remains.

He discovered a new emotion, raw and ugly as a newborn. Standing in the sadness and the slaughter, anger bloomed in his heart. If a wolf can be said to harbor vengeance, this whelp found it and sheltered it. One day, he would avenge his parents and siblings. He would kill the dinosaurs who killed his family. He tucked his vengeance close to his heart where others could not see because it was all his own and nobody else's.

His stomach growled audibly.

Vengeance could not be fed on hatred alone. The puppy ran to the bottom of the mountain, far from his family's corpses. There, he located a dead elk half-submerged in the Seven Graves River. A less-than-ideal introduction to meat, but carrion was sustenance. Cautiously, he approached the body of the dead elk. He stopped and smelled the wind like his family elders did. He wasn't sure what he was smelling for, but he it was an important part of the process. Smelling nothing, the puppy moved forward, slowly at first, but then running. His stomach pangs were terrible. They controlled him.

He tore into the flesh. He'd never tasted elk before. The meat was cold and difficult to chew, but that didn't matter to him. Elk meat was the best thing he'd ever tasted. Much better than milk and regurgitated gopher. Most important of all, the nourishment was vital. He ripped a thin ribbon of meat from the elk's rib cage and chewed it voraciously, moving the meat around in his mouth and then swallowing it down. His youthful blue eyes sparkled. He took another bite.

Behind the lone wolf, two small Compsognathus dinosaurs noticed the mammal bounding through the grass. They turned and watched him stop at the water's edge. They licked their mouths hungrily. The circle of life was about to cycle to them. They raised their green claws. Ever so quietly, they approached the unsuspecting puppy.

The wolfling stopped eating and sniffed the wind, but he didn't smell the Compys. The summer breezes were funneling off the river and blowing toward the predators. The wolf was obliviously downwind of them.

The dinosaurs paused, their eager claws pulsating. He was larger than their usual diet of lizards and field mice, but he was soft and fluffy. An easy target in a harsh environment. The only movement was their eyes, which ever-so-slowly signaled to each other that the kill was about to happen. When the puppy stopped sniffing, the pair of Compys closed within inches of him, ready to strike. He was just on the other side of the grass, completely unaware.

Finally within reach, the Compys pounced. However, their claws caught nothing but air. The lone wolf cub had disappeared. But where to?

A summer frog had caught the hungry pup's eye. Live meat trumped long-dead meat any day. He jumped on it at the same moment the Compys jumped for him. The Compys snarled their frustration at the missed opportunity. Their sounds gave them away.

Hearing the Compys, the young wolfling sprinted through the high grass, the strip of elk meat jangling in his mouth. He was terrified. He'd never encountered Compys before. They weren't that much bigger than him, about the size of an overgrown chicken, but there were two of them, and he was learning that he was not only ignorant but also quite naive.

The Compys chased the puppy through the field, hissing. One cut left while the other stayed on the puppy's heels, driving the unsuspecting wolf to his doom. The little ball of fluff would have no chance against these prehistoric predators.

The puppy yipped his fear, hoping that his mother would rescue him, and knowing at the same time that nobody was coming for him. He was alone in this mean world, and his odds of survival were dwindling. He either had to grow up fast or become somebody else's meal.

The Compys had gone silent. The puppy no longer heard them running in the grass. He turned around to look. The grass waved back at him. Where had they gone? He lifted his head from side to side. His ears still weren't completely erect yet. The tips of his ears flopped onto his round face.

WHAM! The Compy hit him hard, rolling him over and clawing at him.

He was a puppy, but he wasn't defenseless. He snapped at the Compy's neck.

The wolf caught the Compy's neck in his jaw, but his jaw muscles weren't strong enough to inflict serious damage with his new teeth. The Compy shoved him off its body. As the wolf rolled, the second Compy came up beside the first and slashed at the puppy's face, narrowly missing the puppy's eye but gouging a hole in the wolf's ear.

The wolf threatened them as best he could, but his little puppy voice was endearing rather than menacing, and blood was dripping from his torn ear. The Compys didn't buy it. They raised their claws and approached for the final kill.

WHUD! The thick foot of the Majungasaurus slammed down on the Compys. Much smaller than a T. Rex, the Majungasaurus was still a terrific ambush predator. It picked apart the first Compy in its claws, biting its head off, then its arms. The second Compy hissed angrily. The Majungasaurus pressed down on the Compy, crushing its ribs under the weight of its foot.

The wolf puppy retreated into the high grass. There was a lesson to be learned about ambush predators and dinosaurs. In the land of giants, there was always a bigger threat, but more importantly, he could use them to his advantage.

***

The puppy needed a place to hide. The grass was poor protection from rapacious dinosaurs, and he didn't trust hiding among the rocks along the riverbanks. And while it was probably the best place, he couldn't bear to return to the high mountain where his family's bodies lay.

That left the woods at the far end of the valley floor. The sun rose and fell before the puppy arrived. He had to be very quiet and very wary. He did not want any of the other dinosaurs to discover him. So the wolfling snuck along the edge of the valley, careful to avoid the large-horned and long-necked herbivores roaming there. Several times, the puppy ducked into the grass so as not to be seen by the pterosaurs flying overhead, searching for small vertebrates to pick off the ground.

By nightfall he'd journeyed all the way across the valley and into the forest. His stomach was rumbling again, and he was thirsty. He did not know what to do to fix the hole in his stomach. He needed a place to hide.

In a half-fallen tree with two small branches sticking out, he found a hollow among the roots. The tree had been knocked half-way over, but it was not dead yet. The wolf puppy slid between the upturned roots. He chased his tail three times, then laid down and began moving the leaves out of his way. The leaves formed a fragile little door at the end of his hollow.

His first night alone, the puppy thought of his litter mates. When they were hungry or scared or thirsty, they yowled for their mama to come and bring them food or make the bad shadows go away. He thought of food, too. When his brothers and sisters returned from the hunt, their regurgitated gopher was plenty to fill his stomach. Although he liked the taste of elk better, he wouldn't turn his nose up to digested gopher. They were fat and round and easy to tear apart.

The puppy yawned because he was anxious and very sleepy. He could not keep his eyes open. Goodbye gophers, and goodbye littermates. He was the lone surviving member of the New Profanity Mountain Pack. His hide was gray, and his eyes were blue. One ear had a hole pierced in it. Utterly alone in the world and surrounded by the deadliest predators to ever walk the Earth, the wolfling began his first solo slumber.

***

Morning brought coarse winds and a bigger rumble in his stomach. He needed to eat soon or perish. The wolf pushed aside his meager leaf door and scampered down into the valley. He made his way slowly back across the valley floor to the river, cautious that no Compys were near. He lapped up as much cold water as he could drink. It was a temporary respite from the gnawing sensation in his gut. His plan was to follow his nose back to the dead elk.

A grasshopper sat on a blade of grass, cleaning itself. Beggars cannot be choosers. He snapped at the meager grasshopper, but it was too quick for him. Oh, well. He'd have to look elsewhere for another meal.

From somewhere in the distance, a great roar ignited the air like lightning. Thunder followed, loud and rampaging. An avalanche of sound rushed toward the river and the wolf.

The little puppy ran from side to side in a near panic. Where to go? What to do? If his mother or father were there, they could guide him and show him what to do. Now it was up to him to make the decision. There was the water. Was it too deep? He'd never traversed a river before, but today was his day. He plunged into the river and swam out to its deepest depths.

The puppy knew nothing of currents and rapids. The waters swept him away. He yipped for assistance and dog-paddled with all his might, but he was too tiny. His head went under for a moment, but then he bobbed back up. His win was momentary. The upcoming riffle, full of jagged boulders, appeared like teeth in the foaming water. The river prepared to devour another victim.

Two giants staggered into the river. One was a long-necked Apatosaurus. Its footsteps were the thunder in the wolf's ears. It squared up in the river, nearly crushing the puppy with its churning legs. The wolf swirled around and around. One of the waves from the giant's stomping lifted him over the rocks and dumped him back ashore.

The wolf choked out water and shook his fur coat. Lines of water arced in the air and splattered in the riverside.

A hideous creature reared its head from the grass directly in front of the puppy. Small, black horns jutted from in front of the eyes of an otherwise rust-colored body. The Allosaurus opened its mouth so wide, twenty adult wolves could have fit into its jaws. The Allosaurus's eyes were trained on the little wolf pup.

The wolf lifted his head and tried to growl more menacingly than it had with the Compys. The Allosaurus didn't hear. Behind the wolf, the Apatosaurus raised its neck as high as possible. The Apatosaurus showed its long tail with the thin, colorful fleshy end. The tail made a cracking sound as it whipped it over and over, trying to draw the Allosaurus's attention.

This Allosaurus wasn't fooled. The meat eater jumped at the Apatosaurus, sinking its mouth into the Apatosaurus's side and ripping at its flesh. The Apatosaurus bucked. One hit from its leg would kill the Allosaurus, but the carnivore didn't give up. It hung on tight to the belly like a rock climber on wet rocks. It would not let go.

The Apatosaurus was in so much pain, it whipped its head around to snap at the Allosaurus' jaws, but this is exactly what the Allosaurus wanted. When the head was close enough, the meat eater released his clamp on the dinosaur's belly. Blood splashed in the water below.

The gargantuan herbivore moaned.

The Allosaurus grabbed onto that thick cord of neck and bit down hard with its wide jaws. The Apatosaurus moaned. It swung its neck, but that was a fatal mistake. The creature's wild movements only tore at its neck more. It could feel its windpipe crushing under the pressure of the Allosaurus' tight grip. The Allosaurus did not give up. It squeezed harder and harder until the Apatosaurus began choking on its own blood. Frothy blood dribbled down its nose. Impotently, it kicked at the Allosaurus, but it had neither the reach nor the strength.

The long neck slumped on all fours and groaned. Its tongue hung out of its mouth. Its tail stopped squirming. Then the Allosaurus severed the neck, which it flipped around casually in the river like a meat club before giving it up and licking the beast's belly.

The food chain in Dinosaur Falls Wildlife Restricted Area is fickle. All kills will lengthen the lifetime of any carnivore, so no kill is complete until it is consumed, and every other predator knows this. As the Apatosaurus died, ravens swarmed down from the trees, landing on the carcass. Within minutes two more Allosauruses showed up, looking for dinner. The hunter had to stake his claim to his own kill. He hissed a warning to the other two of its kind. They were juveniles with small horns. When they ventured too close, he bit them on the nose and they ran off into the nearby trees.

After ten minutes of back and forth, the juvenile Allosauruses finally gave up on the Apatosaurus. The hunter returned to his kill. He snapped at the ravens, and they flew far enough away to avoid becoming hors d'oeuvres.

The wolfling studied all these interactions, which were in their own way as subtle and strategic as any dinner party setting in a Jane Austen romance. If only the puppy were literate.

The puppy chose a different tactic. Slowly, he approached the decapitated neck, head down to demonstrate he was no threat. The neck cavity was all bone and sinew. The Allosaurus growled while stuffing his face. He was an eating machine. Hide, muscle, and fat all went down his throat indiscriminately in great gulps.

The puppy didn't have much choice. He kept his head bowed and approached the far side of the dead Apatosaurus. There was much risk for him here. He was exposed to the Allosaurus, and he could be swept away by the current again.

But his hunger was great and terrible.

The Allosaurus ripped a chunk of meat from the Apatosaurus's belly and gulped it down savagely. The little wolf puppy attacked the Apatosaurus's neck. The Allosaurus did not stop him. In this way, the puppy ate his fill and developed his first taste for dinosaur at the same time.

After a meal of bone and sinew, which was tough on his teeth, the wolf tried for a piece of the actual Apatosaurus instead of just its severed head. Slowly, he approached the carcass. The giant meat eater watched him with one horned eye. When the wolf pup got close enough, the Allosaurus attacked. He snapped his mouth, catching only air.

The wolf ran up the riverside. Loud, pounding steps followed him. He knew he didn't have long before the Allosaurus's jaws reached around him. The puppy searched frantically for a place to hide. He cut into the fields and nearly tripped over a small burrow. The wolf dove into the burrow, legs scratching and pawing to climb deeper into the ground.

As he did, the Allosaurus slammed into the ground above. It felt to the puppy like a great earthquake was smashing around him. The Allosaurus pawed at the ground with his back legs, digging up the wolf. The wolf yipped as he flew through the air. The Allosaurus bit at him but missed again. The wolf lunged back into the ground, digging deeper.

The Allosaurus churned at the Earth. Great chunks of dirt and rock disappeared around the wolf, but then it stopped. The wolf, heart pounding, sat in the roots and dirt and stopped, too. Was the dinosaur searching for him?

No, it was returning to the kill. He could hear the steps fading away. Two more electric growls told the wolf pup that the young Allosauruses had returned. The hunter had bigger problems now.

As did the badger snarling at him. The wolf retreated. The badger charged, snapping and snarling. It was as mean as the Allosaurus and just as willing to make a meal out of the unsuspecting puppy.

The wolf whelp pushed backwards and hopped out of the burrow, but not before the badger could bite off another piece of his ear.

The puppy howled in pain.

Topside, he saw the Allosauruses fighting. He decided his belly was full enough. He slunk the rest of the way to his home in the tree stump and quietly sobbed himself to sleep.

CHAPTER TWO

The lone wolf pushed and shoved his way out of the broken tree's roots. The tree stump gently rocked in the soft earth.

The giant wolf's head poked out of his den. He had grown since summer, thriving on his diet of dinosaur meat. The wolf was taller and stronger than any other wolf, even than his mother. His blue eyes had transformed into sleek, golden discs. A full crest of hair flushed from his cheeks.

He stretched his long, lean body in the morning light. Among the rocks beside the tree, three Compys had not seen the wolf's den hidden under the snow. They scampered out of his way. He clamped one in his jaws, crunching its bones and swallowing it whole. Yes, much had changed since last summer.

He was no longer a stranger in a strange land anymore. He'd gained a wealth of information about his unique environment and the new creatures that populated its mountains.

The wolf darted among the conifers bordering the valley and slinked through the snow and grass down to the Seven Graves River, marking his territory as he went. He halted when a pack of Allosauruses entered the valley. The wolf's damaged ears stood erect as he paused to watch them.

The wolf stalked dinosaurs in the restricted area.

The Allosauruses were not coming for him. As the wolf suspected, the Allosauruses approached the herds to the south. Eight Apatosauruses saw the predators first and flapped warning snaps with the ends of their tails, alerting the other herbivores. The long necks then positioned themselves behind a pair of Ankylosauruses and a lone Stegosaurus.

The large meat eaters stopped and considered this maneuver. They desired fresh Apatosaurus meat. One dead Apatosaurus could feed them for weeks. Though the large sauropods were not to be taken lightly, the other dinosaurs were armed with vicious weapons and were far more dangerous. In general, Allosauruses did not hunt the herbivores with horns and clubs and armor. In robust months, they targeted easier prey, but lean winter months led to empty stomachs and desperate minds. If the Allosauruses did not eat, they would not survive to spring.

How to separate the long necks from the armored? The meat eaters divided, two going one direction and the third moving farther into the valley. Their hope was to take turns attacking from different angles. By working together, they could scare an Apatosaurus from leaving the safe confines of its deadlier mates.

The wolf watched this guerilla warfare and waited for his moment. Three times the Allosauruses attacked the strange herd, and three times the dinosaurs refused to separate. The Ankylosauruses and Stegosaurus remained between them and their prize.

The lone wolf laid down in frustration. The standoff was intolerable, and he was hungry, too. Since he wasn't anywhere near the largest predator in Dinosaur Falls, he had to be opportunistic and at all times, patient. Finally, though, his patience paid off when one of the Ankylosauruses rumbled right instead of left. The armored female was not the favorite choice of the Allosauruses, but time and energy were not on their side. They needed to end this pursuit soon or give up in futility. Such an act might commit one of them to starvation.

The Allosauruses formed a triangle around the Ankylosaurus. They attempted to force her to run, to tire her out, but the Ankylosaurus stood her ground. A baby Ankylosaur appeared underneath her armor. This mother wasn't running. She waved her massive clubbed tail warningly at the meat eaters. Sinister eyes watched her baby and licked their lips. The game had changed.

The wolf perked up.

Mama's tail swooshed long and low, arcing like a sickle through the grass. The Allosauruses jumped out of its reach. Mama wailed a piercing warning. The Allosauruses screamed back at her threat.

The wolf crawled through the high grass, his ears fully erect, every fiber of his muscular body tuned in to the battle. He moved slowly, one paw at a time, to remain undetected by the much larger predators.

Far from the mother's fight, the rest of the dinosaurs lumbered away. The only one to remain was the male Ankylosaurus. He moaned to his mate from the mountainside but dared not come closer to the Allosauruses.

The wolf sped up. All four feet still hit the ground, but in the quietest, quickest canter possible. Completely undetected, he was a stealth bomber on a raid, swooping in for the strafing.

The armored Ankylosaurus feinted with her tail. The forward-most Allosaurus took the bait and jumped in for the baby. With a nasty snarl, the Ankylosaurus swung. Her tail slammed into the Allosaurus's head. A large crack rang out across the valley.

Skull bone crumbled and split. Air sacs burst. Brains splattered, and the Allosaurus was dead before its head painted the ground. The body of the Allosaurus flipped around sideways, spraying blood, then came to a lifeless thud beside the clubber. For extra emphasis, Mama slammed her bloody tail into the bowl that was the Allosaurus's broken skull.

The two remaining Allosaurus dinosaurs stood back. Their pack member lay on the ground, the little horns in front of his eyes split into jarring angles. This no longer seemed fair, and they weren't sure the baby was worth the risk.

The Ankylosaurus roared another warning to the two bachelors. She sounded like one of the giant mechanical birds that flew above the clouds. Her intent was clear. Any who came near her or her baby would meet the same fate.

This was the moment!

The wolf swooped in, flying under the Ankylosaurus's bony protrusions while she was distracted. He knew he had one shot at this. He bit down tight onto the fleshy meat between one of the baby's legs. The baby bawled like any calf, mammalian or dinosaurian, that is suddenly attacked by a wolf. The irony of this hunt was not lost on the wolf. Not too long ago, he had been the baby being chased for slaughter. The wolf tugged hard against the baby Ankylosaurus's groin, but the baby Ank did not budge. It dug its feet into the ground.

Mama heard this commotion and turned to the lone wolf. She snapped at him, but by then the Allosauruses had jumped onto her plate-covered back. They curled their necks around her body, and bit at her fleshy undersides.

The mother swung her mighty club, but the meat eaters were too close to be effective. The club was not made to slam down on her back. So Mama squatted down, trapping her baby, and the wolf, under her mighty armored shell. This did not have the effect she wanted because she essentially trapped her baby with the lone wolf. The wolf ripped at her baby's skin. The baby screamed in pain. Panicking, Mama stood and ran. The baby ran beside her, the wolf bouncing in the dirt.

A giant club came out of nowhere and swung at the wolf. He released the baby.

Father had come to the rescue. He snarled with metallic hate in his voice. He swung his clubbed tail. The wolf was so small and nimble, the father had a difficult time hitting him. The wolf hopped over the male

Ankylosaurus's even heavier club. The heavy club swung side to side slowly, giving the wolf enough time to jump on top of the male Ank's armored back.

The father yelled angrily. This confrontation wasn't supposed to work this way. He was used to much larger, more lumbering creatures.

The lone wolf did not care. He ran the length of the dinosaur's back and chomped on the male's neck. The dinosaur raged against him, swiveling his head from side to side. But the wolf knew just when to let go so as not to be smashed between the creature's massive horns and plates. He bit and snapped and bit and snapped until his fangs found tender arteries. Arterial blood spewed hot and wet in the cold winter. The male fell in the grass.

The father Ank's sacrifice was not without some victory.

Mama and her baby ran back to the herd. The wolf wasn't confident the Ank baby would survive the night. The wounds were too deep. The lone wolf would return and check on the baby after the moon rose. For now, though, he had this kill, but he had to be quick. He stuck his maw deep into the Ankylosaurus's hot muscle. He pulled and ripped and swallowed meat quickly.

When the two Allosauruses approached the wolf's kill, he knew what to do. He'd learned the intricacies of guarding the kill. He growled back at them. He raised his hackles and bared his teeth. And when that didn't work, he charged the two titans, all teeth and bite. Although the giant meat eaters outweighed him by several orders of magnitude, they scattered like ravens. One-ton nightmares being chased off by an adolescent wolf.

Briefly, the dinosaurs considered a different approach. They hissed at each other and then the wolf, showing him their displeasure, and then alerting him of their intention. They walked up to the wolf that was swallowing huge chunks of dinosaur meat.

Again, the comparatively smaller wolf chased them off. He was able to do this because in this instance, he was not a wolf. He was an Ankylosaurus killer - something they were not. This fact was the only thing keeping the Allosauruses away from *his* kill. The wolf smiled. He was a wolverine chasing off grizzly bears!

Too quickly, the Allosauruses changed their minds. The wolf snapped and snarled, but the colossal, horned carnivores didn't run. They opened their mouths to show the wolf they could swallow an entire pack in one bite. The rust-colored beasts began hunting the wolf.

The wolf gave up the bluff and retreated. Usually the dinosaurs gave up quickly, but these two were different. Young bachelors, they wanted a piece of him. They chased the wolf back across the fields.

The wolf had experience being chased by large theropods. He remembered the badger hole. Surely the badger was dead by now. He dove for the familiar hole.

Problem was, only half his body made it into the small hole. The back half endeared itself to the outside world and made an irresistible bull's eye target to the Jurassic-sized predators.

Realizing his mistake, the wolf yelped. He pushed back out and shook the dirt off his head fur. An Allosaurus thundered behind him and snipped at his leg. The wolf jumped out of the way, flying almost straight into the open mouth of the second Allosaurus.

The wolf bit down on the Allosaurus's snout. The dinosaur howled painfully as it shook him off.

Too close!

The wolf rolled into a run and raced for the steep mountainside, where the giant carnivores hesitated to follow. He left them in a dirt wave. He was so much faster than them, they didn't stand a chance. Laughing, he ran a circle around the giant meat-eating nightmares as they wandered back to the fresh corpse of the Ankylosaurus. They lunged at the wolf, but he was nowhere near them. This was play. He zig-zagged around the two-legs until he was tired and bored, and then he wandered out of their range.

From a rocky perch, he watched them eat. This was the natural law of living among dinosaurs. Often bigger and deadlier predators overtook his kill. But the belly of a wolf is much smaller than the belly of an Allosaurus, and he was a fast eater. His belly full, he watched the Allosauruses devour his hard-fought cornucopia of muscles, fat, and entrails.

He missed regurgitated gopher.

CHAPTER THREE

The wolf slept through the night and didn't check on the Ankylosaurus baby. Instead, he woke late, long past sunrise. By then, cold sunlight made the early morning snow glisten.

The stump bulged outward as he climbed from his shelter. He shivered as he yawned and stretched. The leaves and branches weren't insulating him the way they did when he was younger. He watched the movements of the different herds of carnivores and herbivores. The bachelor Allosauruses stood under the trees. Their vacant eyes drifted languidly to the herbivores, lacking any motivation.

The wolf waited a long time for the Allosauruses to make a move. His life depended on Allosaurus hunts.

He had an idea. It was not the first time he'd had this idea, but it was the first time he'd decided to follow this instinct. The bachelor herd was missing its third Allosar since he'd been clobbered the day before. Perhaps the wolf could be that third?

It made sense. He'd seen the herbivores living this way all year. Long necked beasts alerted the other species of dinosaurs to the threat, and then they stayed far behind the Ankylosauruses, Triceratops, and even Stegosauruses. If the prey could do it, why not the predators?

Something akin to hope bloomed in the dark pit of the wolf's soul. He'd lived a lonely life, and he'd found success, excelling in his abilities and taming this new wilderness with all its strange and mysterious creatures. Yet since the day of the raptors, the one thing he never regained was a packmate. These Allosaurus creatures certainly behaved like packmates. Perhaps he could convince them to let him join their pack, if he could prove his use.

He would have to wait.

Three days later, he noticed the two Allosaurus bachelors' movements becoming more aggressive. They began watching the herds more diligently. The wolf decided it was time.

The lone wolf wandered through the forest, his nose dipping down to test the scents of various footprints. After wandering through the conifers for some time, he found the scent he wanted and tracked it through the trees. He had to be careful. He did not know the forest as well as he did the valley. There were many predators he did not recognize. Some had horns, and others had giant, cavernous mouths. He needed to avoid them all until he could understand them better.

The wolf jogged through the trees, following the large prints in the snow. He jumped over frosted logs and crossed ravines until he finally caught up to them.

The Nodosaurs were shorter and smaller than the Ankylosauruses he hunted yesterday. Much smaller nubs covered their reddish backs. Short horns adorned their heads, and their tails were not weaponized like a Stegosaurus or Ank. The tail simply tapered off.

Relative to the fully armored tank that he'd fought yesterday, Nodosaurs were vulnerable targets. But for what they lacked in plates, they made up in speed. Nodosaurs could easily outrun Anks.

For the Allosauruses, their speed was a very real problem, but for the wolf, their speed was a non-factor. All large dinosaurs were slow. What was fifteen or twenty miles an hour when you could run twenty miles an hour for *hours*, and you could sprint at thirty to thirty-five?

The wolf made his presence known, standing up tall and watching the herd. The shadow of his head slid across the backs of the Nodosaurs. Six adults and one calf lifted their heads in his direction. The other calves, unaware, munched on forest ferns.

The wolf pushed toward them. This herd had never encountered a wolf. They didn't know what to do with him, but as herbivores, they understood claws and fangs. They didn't like the idea of him hanging around. So the two males bellowed, and the herd ambled away.

They were walking up into the mountain forests. The wolf needed them down in the valley with the Allosaurus bachelors.

The lone wolf stole around to the far side of the herd, galloping low to the ground, then popping up on their right. He was closer than the first time he appeared.

A nearby female, not thirty yards from him, barked. The wolf barked back. The two male Nodosaurs stepped forward and flicked their ears at him and waved their tails.

Not far away, a boulder rested in the snow. The wolf scurried to the far side of the boulder. Several smaller rocks and a crisscrossed log lay against the far side of the boulder. The wolf climbed the log and rocks to the top of the boulder. He pushed his chest out. His hackles stood on end. He scanned the herd as he bared his shiny teeth. His tail flicked eagerly behind him. He was the predator. He was the killer. He allowed the wind to communicate the scent of meat and blood that emanated from his mouth, his fur, and his anus. He was the one the shepherd feared, and *they were the flock.*

The two males did not trust this strange new predator in the forest. He was small, but fearsome and dangerous. The Nodosaurs turned and began trotting down to the valley.

The wolf waited until the right moment, then ran behind the herd, yipping excitedly. The Nodosaurs ran faster. Great billows of snow rose behind them, and for a moment the wolf was lost in the kick-up. He used the cover to sprint to the side and appear parallel to them.

The Nodosaurs rumbled into the valley, a walking mountain of mass and noise. The wolf cried out happily. His plan was working. He remembered the location of the Allosaurus bachelors. He steered the Nodosaurs toward them, barking with all the happiness and joy of the hunt.

In the distance, Allosauruses crouched under the trees.

Wait, he wanted to tell them. *Not yet.*

The Allosauruses did not move. Their muscles tensed, but they remained in their position, like arrows drawn across the bow waiting to be released.

The lone wolf pushed against the side of the herd wall. The Nodosaurs reacted in kind, veering toward the Allosauruses.

Now!

The wolf barked loudly at the two meat eaters. *Attack!*

The carnivores lingered as motionless as statues. *Why weren't they attacking? What were they waiting for? I practically ran them right beside you!*

The wolf sprinted ahead of the Nodosaur herd and attempted to alter their course again. He popped up from the grass less than twenty yards from the charging Nodosaurs.

They didn't stop.

The wolf's ears slunk. In English, the pinned back ears could be interpreted as any number of curse words. He immediately regretted his ploy. The herd was charging right at him!

Six animals, each weighing over a thousand pounds, stormed through the snow, barking and screaming in fear. They ran right over him.

The wolf jumped side to side, dodging Nodosaurs like they were boulders crashing down a mountainside. One stomped his foot. The wolf gritted his teeth and fought the desire to bite back. His goal was not to kill. He was trying to convince the Allosauruses to kill. He was training them to work in his pack.

A Nodosaur bumped him lightly, but a moving, massive body covered in armored plates hitting a much smaller, fleshier one causes a lot of pain to the smaller body. The wolf yelped as he rolled away from the herd.

He growled in frustration at the two young bachelors. This wasn't working. The two "different lizards" (as their name meant in Latin) remained under the trees.

The wolf ran parallel to the herd. Last chance. He didn't pop up but emerged from the grass like a shark's fin cutting through the surf. The Nodosaurs turned once more and charged back toward the Seven Graves River. Yes! He steered them straight at the Allosaurus dinosaurs.

The Nodosaurs shot through the forest. Finally, the Allosauruses lunged at the Nodosaurs. Completely surprised by the ambush, the "Nods" were easy prey. The Allosaurus bachelors picked off one old female and a young calf. Both were so tired from all the running, they collapsed and gave up as the wide jaws of the Allosauruses grabbed them.

The lone wolf came barking and yipping his encouragement to the Allosaurus bachelors. He was downright gleeful. It worked!

Tail wagging, he ran up close to the meat eaters. In the distance, the Nodosaurs plowed into the river. They huddled in the center of the rushing waters and waited for the devil dog to disappear.

The wolf barked excitedly at the two Allosauruses, but they didn't react the way he hoped. Instead of wagging their tails, or at least eating hungrily, they growled at the wolf like he was trying to take the kill they had earned. *Go away, you. This is our kill. You did a lousy job chasing those armor-plated meat buckets, and now they are ours.*

When the wolf didn't run away but kept wagging its damn tail and yipping, they chased the wolf back up the valley. Just like the last time, the wolf easily outlasted the two-legs. He circled around to a safe distance and watched them eat greedily.

The lone wolf stewed for a while.

Allosauruses did not make good pack mates, he concluded. The wolf needed to look elsewhere for companionship.

CHAPTER FOUR

The wolf set out the next day to find a new pack. First, he scavenged the leftovers from the Nodosaur kill, then he set foot toward the mountains away from New Profanity. There was so much expanse in Dinosaur Falls and such diverse ecosystems, he could run for days and never leave it.

Certainly, somewhere he would find his pack.

As he walked, his foot landed on top of an old footprint he made running up and down the fields in the summer. He was so much smaller back then. He was an adult wolf now. Time to start acting like one.

The wolf wandered along several animal trails that delivered him to the top of a narrow, crested ridge. Gray granite rocks formed a two-foot ledge exposed to the sun and weather. The ledge curled convexly to either side, forming a large semi-circular shape between blunted, snow-covered peaks. From this ridge he looked behind him to the valley he knew. This was the fullest extent of his territory. Take one more step, and he was in a new world.

Beyond lay a section of the restricted area called The Devil's Cauldron. Formed by glaciers eons ago, this cirque was visually arresting. Rivers, lakes, and narrow canyons spiraled and snaked in dazzling shapes. The sun reflected off the waters, giving a luminescence to the spirals that stood out against the dark forests and plains.

Winged Dimorphodons dove from the sides of the Devil's Cauldron. These "Wolves of the Sky" swooshed over the trees, scouring for prey. Long-necked Brachiosaurs moved among the treetops below.

The wolf looked around, organized his bearings, then stepped off the Cauldron's rim.

He searched up and down the draws on the far side of the ridgeline. He'd never ventured this far from his root burrow. Wolves were nomadic predators by nature, and the lone wolf often felt the tug of distant lands pulling at his soul, but he was alone and without a pack to support him. Travel was risky. He was but one fleshy carnivore minus frills, horns, scales, or feathers to protect him. The danger was high, but so was the need for a pack.

If he caught the scent of several large animals, he snuck up on them and studied the dinosaurs to determine if they would be a good fit for his pack. Most of the dinosaurs he encountered were a completely new species for him, and the wolf did not have a parent to show him the ropes or discriminate between predator and prey. Sometimes he found a grouping of herbivores, such as humpbacked Draconyx or Iguanodons. Once he nearly ran into ten brightly colored Stegosauruses, and another time he watched from atop a rocky ledge as titan-sized Brachiosaurs galumphed through the forest.

At Devil's Cauldron Lake the wolf nearly met certain disaster when he walked straight into the waiting jaws of a hidden Spinosaurus. If not for the Spinosaurus's overeager hunger, he would have become lunch. He hadn't seen the blazing eyes burning with hunger or the large floating log that was the creature's mouth. The wolf crept along the lake's banks, oblivious to the giant fin approaching behind him. Everything in Dinosaur Falls was gigantic. The fin was no exception. The Spinosaurus lunged too quickly, though. If it had been more patient and crept a little closer, the young wolf would have had no chance of escaping. But the Spinosaurus hadn't eaten in days. That overeager drive betrayed the creature. The sailfin wiggled back and forth. A massive tail propelled the fifteen-thousand-pound body across the lake in a serpentine motion. The wolf easily scuttled out of the kill zone of the world's largest predator. After that, the wolf stayed away from the lake's shores.

Deeper into the mountains the wolf willed himself, always hoping to find a new pack. He hunted small dinosaurs and the occasional mammal to tide over his hunger.

Near a draw called the Black Gate, the large wolf detected the scent of a multitude of predators. Many days had passed wandering the wintry woods since he encountered the Spinosaurus. The tug in his heart was growing more powerful with each day. He had to find these predators.

As he neared them, the wolf heard a loud commotion, like a sea of grackles cawing at each other. He peeked over a log, keeping his mutilated ears close to his scalp so as not to be seen. On the other side of a large oak log stood hundreds of tiny bird-like dinosaurs, called Coelophysis. They weren't forty pounds each, but they were thin and fast, and their mouths were full of recurved, serrated teeth. He didn't want to tempt them, so he hunched low and backpedaled out of their way.

Wolves are predators of grace, ballerinas with fangs. He backed away on his soft feet without betraying his identity or location. He was almost away when he slipped on a hidden sheet of ice and landed with a thud on the ground.

The entire herd went dead silent instantly. They were invisible to him on the other side of the log.

For a moment the wolf believed he'd been lucky and eluded detection. Then all at once they rushed him, flooding over the log. The wolf retreated as fast as his legs could carry him, but these little terrors were faster than most dinosaurs he'd encountered.

They were also trying to outflank him. Coelophysises outgained him on the side, where the terrain was easier to run.

The wolf barked at the flankers. He couldn't believe his luck. He finally found a pack of predators, and they were trying to hunt *him*. He ran back down Black Gate draw, but the Coelophsysises followed with passion. It was like an army of over-sized ants running after him. Because they could smell him and see him, they wouldn't give up the chase. He had to outrun them or outthink them.

The flankers pushed in toward his sides. They were driving him to the ridgeline. Steep cliff banks, twenty to fifty feet deep, cut the side of the ridge. The little monsters intended to force him over. He had to think of a solution quick.

Up ahead, a V-shaped figure emerged from the forest. The wolf ran toward it. He couldn't quite make it out. The figure lay in shadow.

Behind him surged the mass of biting, snapping Coelophysises. The predatorial herd closed in on him. Pretty soon, he would have to choose between confronting the herd or jumping off the ledge. Neither option felt survivable.

Out of the darkness, the V-shaped figure finally took shape and meaning. The blackened tree bent in half by a lightning strike would be his deliverance. He'd climb the tree and out of their way. It was his only move.

The wolf leaped up the fallen log and turned to laugh, but the Coelophysises ran right up the tree after him. The wolf never considered dinosaurs could climb trees. He couldn't, so why should they?

Well, Coelophysis was no Allosaurus or Stegosaurus. Unlike those giants, they were light and powerful, and they climbed trees expertly. The wolf was beginning to think that these tiny Coelophysises were much more dangerous than the giant predators he'd encountered in the valley.

A horde of little monsters dug their slasher claws into the blackened tree bark and opened their mouths wide.

The wolf abandoned the bent tree as the broken log crashed under the weight of all those narrow bodies. Flankers from both sides swarmed toward him. He landed on a few. Their bites were nowhere near as strong or deadly as his, but there were so many! They quickly ripped little pieces of flesh from his legs and belly. He kicked and bit, but he couldn't stop to fight. There were just too many. They'd overpower him in seconds.

The wolf had to escape. He kept running. What choice did he have? That ledge the dinosaurs were driving him toward approached closer and closer. If he didn't do something real soon, he was going to become a high-diving canine.

Golden eyes swished back and forth, searching desperately for an opening or a path. Anything!

Behind him, the Coelophysis kept up with him like no other dinosaur he'd ever encountered.

It was time to stop running and sprint. The wolf accelerated. His legs flew across the broken rock. The little Coelophysis monsters squawked their indignation. How dare that wolf run faster!

The curtain of teeth and fangs closed shut behind him, narrowly missing him. The wolf pushed himself harder. He leapt over the limestone and turned into a narrow canyon of snow and rock. Belligerent strata frowned down on the wolf, black and gray-hued lines buckled and kinked worse than an electrocardiogram run amok. He crawled behind a boulder and hoped the narrow-mouthed carnivores would rush past him.

They were a freight train rushing along the edge of the canyon, difficult to stop and harder to turn. The wolf smiled. Maybe something was going right for a change.

But then one of the Coelophysis monsters saw him out of the corner of his eye. His little electric thumper of a squawk changed its tone: less ecstatic and more pulsating, like a homing beacon from a scifi monster movie.

"OOhmm-muh-muh-OOhmm-muh-muh-OOhmm…"

That single, insufferable Coelophysis jumped aside of the mob. Before the wolf could snuff out the scout, his family received the communication. They stopped, too, and altered the timbre in their voice while facing the wolf.

All those eyes on him. They twinkled and glowed in the light.

The wolf needed a new plan. He descended into the canyon. Chirping, squawking shouts of bloodlust and glee followed him, first walking, then running.

Hundreds of Coelophysis plunged into the deep behind him. The wolf ran ahead of the impending wave. Down low in the canyon, he could not run as fast. There were too many rocks. They slowed him down. He ducked and dived away from the Coelophysis as they took turns stabbing at him with their beak-like mouths.

The walls turned abruptly, and the wolf came to a crashing halt. In the snow and ice, his body skidded to a stop. What he saw scared him deeply. It frightened him to his core; his tail tucked under his pelvis, and he nearly urinated where he stood.

Large snow-covered mounds in the snow. And for a beautiful second, that's all they were: mounds of snow, and what is there to fear about piles of snow? But then the snow shimmied from the mounds as if an earthquake was reverberating through the canyons; however, this was no earthquake.

Giant heads rose up from the snow in the lower drop. Up and up they went, past the rock he was standing on and high into the air until they consumed the sky and the only thing above him was dinosaurs and canyon walls.

Ancient horrors shook the flurries from their crowns and looked down on the lone wolf. Long teeth, short arms, and massive legs. They'd huddled together for warmth like bloodthirsty penguins in the snow, but there was no mistaking these monsters with penguins. Tyrannosaurus Rexes were the most lethal carnivores to ever roam the Earth.

The momentum of the wave of Coelophysis was not so easily reversed. They tried to stop and turn away from the large herd of Tyrannosaurus Rexes, but mostly they just ended up falling over each other instead.

The closest of the T. Rexes snarled at the wolf and Coelophysis. The "tyrant king" was close enough that the lone wolf could smell the tyrannosaur's breath. His mouth smelled like death incarnate.

The wolf's heart pounded in his chest. He was caught between equally ferocious groups of very small and terrifically large predators.

The T. Rex snapped at the closest Coelophysis. The little monster's wails were silenced in one massive chomp. The Coelophysis simply disappeared. The T. Rex snorted the tiny dinosaur's remains out its nostrils.

The wolf was glad the tyrannosaur had not chosen him.

Looming overhead, the T. Rex growled. The rest of the family, young and old, had all turned to watch the wolf.

The wolf ran back into the unstoppable wave of diminutive predators. He jumped over the first rows of Coelophysis and landed into a pit of rending teeth. The little monsters in the back of the crowd bit and clawed at him, unaware of the alarmed cries of the Coelophysises at the front of the mob. They were like lemmings rushing to the edge of the ice.

With one mighty step, the T. Rex squashed ten Coelophysises. Opportunistic predators have their value when you know your place in the food chain, and the wolf's place was somewhere between the Coelophysis and the Compy but nowhere near the T. Rex.

A tsunamic cacophony rolled from the lower drop. The T. Rexes charged. Their bodies slid over each other as they competed to be the first to the canyon divide. They were like children rushing to the buffet.

As the T. Rexes attacked the Coelophysises, the flood of little teeth quickly realized what was happening. Many fled, but others decided they had no recourse but to attack the T. Rexes. They had the numbers, after all.

The horde swarmed at the first T. Rex, climbing up his legs and biting quickly. The T. Rex bit where he could, but there were so damned many. Once they had reached his arms, he began bleeding profusely from all the gashes in his skin. He stomped and stomped, but they hung on to his legs. He fell, roaring as tiny dinosaurs plucked his eyeballs out.

David felled Goliath. Two prehistoric armies collided.

The wolf knew he had no place in this fight. To the victor would go the spoils, and if he stuck around, those spoils would include one exhausted wolf.

The wolf climbed up the strata, clawing his way to the top. Once over, he looked back down. The T. Rexes moved up and down the canyon, slaughtering the Coelophysis, stomping and gnashing them to bits.

The wolf was grateful to be alive, but he whined a little, sad because he still hadn't secured his pack.

Well, that was nature. One minute the hunter, the next the hunted.

CHAPTER FIVE

The wolf found a shallow cave where he could escape the cold. He curled in a ball and slept deeply. When sunlight finally entered the cave, he resisted opening his eyes. If he were a human, he would have wallowed in self-pity over his failures, but he was born with a short memory for defeat. Dawn had brought a new day with new adversities and mysteries.

His belly argued against sleep until the wolf couldn't fight it anymore. He scurried down into the canyon. The T. Rexes and the Coelophysises were gone. The dead lay as they'd fallen. Necks snapped backwards, ribs crushed, and legs ripped from their bodies. Vultures and Compys picked at the remains. Soon larger species would appear. The wolf had to be quick if he wanted to take advantage of the easy breakfast. He ripped flesh and muscle from bone and scavenged the remains until he was no longer hungry.

He moved on, climbing the mountain, searching for more signs of animal groups. He didn't see any, and his nose told him little more.

Then he smelled something strange. He wasn't sure what to make of this strange smell and tried to ignore it – he'd make better use of scenting for food – but this strange smell bore into his skull. The odor forced its way into the wolf's mind and resurrected raw memories of death and pain. The wolf stopped trying to locate a food source and detoured toward this new smell. He pursued the path, weaving between rocks and ice.

On the far side of the mountains extended a long fence topped with ice-enshrouded razor wire. The trail definitely led him here, so he sniffed the fence line. A narrow slit appeared in the chain link. A stain of feces besmirched the fence. The wolf sniffed the fecal matter, and something clicked inside him. Images of blood and pain and sorrow.

***

A year and a half ago, his mother stood on a flat slab of gray granite and sniffed the hot, summer air. She hoped to detect her mate and their sons returning from the hunt. She needed to eat. The wind carried no message of her family's return. Instead, a strange scent waved in the air. Dinosaurs. Normally, they didn't roam this side of the mountain, but they were near. She whined her anxiety.

Her daughter peeked out of the den. She had the same face as her mother: gray with constellations of tiny white and black spots. She had been watching the five pups while their mother stretched her legs. Her daughter wanted a reassurance that everything was okay.

The mother wolf sniffed the wind a second time. She was the leader here. She would not make a rash decision. Her nose lifted with the wind currents and surveyed the smells. Acorns and pine needles, mostly, but also the dinosaurs. They were meat eaters, too. She knew this because carnivores were chemically different from herbivores. The meat eaters were closing in on the den. Perhaps they were coming up the draw this instant. She whined quietly to her daughter, who stepped out of the den and sniffed the air.

Her daughter's eyes widened. Should they run from the den? The litter was almost old enough to leave. If the dinosaurs had come days later, they might have found an empty den.

How many days later would that have been? Two? Three? One?

Her daughter whined, reminding the mother wolf that now was not the time to speculate. She needed to decide whether to flee or fight. Neither option secured her family. There would be sacrifices. The mother wolf looked to the pups in her den. Too young to fight, but not old enough to run.

Perhaps she should leave them for the dinosaurs to eat and start over with a new litter.

Staying would be a death sentence.

This mother's love was unbinding. She would not leave her pups.

She barked, commanding her daughter to leave. She'd made her decision. The mother wolf wouldn't survive the day, but her daughter could still live. Her daughter looked back at her brothers and sisters. Oversized radar ears and pairs of blue eyes beseeched her to stay.

Her daughter pushed one leg behind her and stiffened in Spartan defiance. She bared her sharp teeth.

The mother rubbed against her. Her daughter would have made a fine pack leader.

The adults carried the pups to the back of the den, which was larger than most wolf dens because the mother was very large for a wolf. She was the biggest wolf in the pack, even bigger than her mate.

The mother wolf coaxed her litter deep into the den. The puppies, detecting the danger, instinctively quieted.

With the litter tucked away, the two females marched out into the hot wind and stood side-by-side. Evening sun beamed between the tree limbs, bathing the rocks in gold and amber light. The wolves waited. They didn't have to wait long.

Dust blew from the mountain. Somewhere, an owl hooted. The invaders were close. She couldn't see them yet, but she could smell them.

The wolves didn't make a sound. They had the confidence of a high-order predator. As a pack, they had a plan for any obstacle they could encounter. A combination of shared history, learned behaviors, and genetic coding propelled them through the world's tribulations. The pack passed down these solutions generationally for thousands of years.

Unfortunately, Velociraptors died out millions of years ago, so the wolves had no effective plans. The two females waited unknowingly for an onslaught more savage than a machine gun and more shocking than an atom bomb.

Pine needles crunched.

The wolves growled. Their hackles raised.

Two Utahraptors charged from the trees, running directly at the wolves. The raptors had a height advantage, but they also ran on two legs, which meant they were easier to knock over. The wolves prepared to jump at them.

The raptors screamed. Their voices sizzled like electric reverb.

The two wolves stood their ground.

A single long claw the shape of a horned moon flashed on each of the raptors' feet. The blood of the pack's males stained those claws.

At the last second, the females jumped at the raptors. As they leapt, three more raptors dropped from the trees at the wolves. The wolves hadn't expected, and never would have thought to expect, a secondary attack from the trees. The wolves rolled along the rocks. Teeth and claws ravaged them. The daughter lost her intestines quickly. A single slash of one of those sickle claws disemboweled her.

But she sprung right back up and bit a Utahraptor's wrist. She shook the arm with enough power to dislocate a human's shoulder. The bite didn't faze the raptor. He was a fighter. The creature pushed toward the young wolf. A second raptor came up behind her and slammed his foot on the daughter's back.

She was too weak to resist his weight. Her hind legs gave out and she collapsed. Still she refused to relinquish the raptor's wrist. There was still some fight in her.

The raptor in front of her reached over, bit her ear off, and swallowed it while she watched.

Still, the daughter would not die. So the raptor gripped her nose in his teeth and twisted it off. Blood gushed from the wound like a broken spigot. While the raptor gobbled her soft nose, the raptor on her back carved up her rear legs.

By then, the daughter was gone.

The mother wolf howled long and hollow. Three raptors had pinned her down and watched the two younger raptors clumsily kill the daughter wolf.

The Utahraptor with his foot on her neck was one of the pack's leaders, and a father to several of her attackers. He barked at the two adolescent raptors. They stopped playing with the dead wolf's body parts.

The father raptor smiled his terrible lizard smile at the mother wolf. Slowly, his horned moon of a claw jabbed at her neck, drawing blood. He was going to make this slow and long.

The mother wolf denied him the satisfaction of locking eyes with her as he brought her to death's door. Instead, her vision longed for the thing she loved most in the world. She watched her den. She willed her whelps to stay where they were. Perhaps the raptors would get bored of so much death and leave.

This would not be that day. The father Utahraptor followed her gaze to the mouth of the den. His smile was particularly cruel. Her eyes betrayed her. He barked a command to the adolescents: kill the pups.

The mother wolf squirmed. She howled plaintively.

She was bigger and stronger than any wolf in the mountains, and she was prepared to die to save her pups. She pushed up. The father raptor shoved his foot down with all his strength, but still she forced herself up, lifting him off the ground. She was bleeding and tired, but these were her pups, and she was going to protect them with her last breath. As soon as she was on her feet, she twisted her body and slipped out of the Utahraptor's grip. She barked at the puppies in her den to run.

She snapped at the closest raptor. It danced easily out of her reach.

The third raptor jumped on her back and dug into her side with his wicked sickles. He grabbed her by the neck and bit down on her shoulder. The mother wolf bucked up and down to knock him off, but the raptor's "spurs" had popped the flesh in front of her hips.

As she railed futilely, five puppies charged out of the den in a last-ditch effort to escape. They jumped over the two adolescent raptors. One pup was caught in mid-air and brained against the rocks. Another got maybe two feet from the den before the second adolescent raptor jumped on him. He raked the puppy up and down with his claws. The puppy cried out and died.

The mother wolf sensed the darkness swirling around her. Whatever angels watch over wolves attended her spirit as she slowly faded. She was already so very, very exhausted. She refused to lay down and sleep, though. She roared her final war cry as she jumped at the father raptor. He slit her throat, cutting her off in mid-roar.

Three scared, yipping wolf puppies bolted into the rocky ledges of New Profanity Peak. The raptors picked them off like fruit from a tree, snatching them from the rocks and sometimes twisting their heads from their bodies like they were screwed on. First one was gone, then the second. A raptor reached for the third, a gray larger than the other pups. He slashed this one, but its hide didn't cut as easily as the others. It squirmed in his hands and kicked him in the face. The raptor let go, and the wolf leaped out over the ledge. The puppy's body bounced from rock to rock, falling so far down the mountainside that it was impossible for him to survive. He landed on a narrow ledge twenty feet below.

The five raptors peered over the side of the mountain at the wolf pup. They watched for a long minute. The pup's body didn't move. His legs jutted out like he'd been electrocuted. Bored, the raptors devoured his soft litter mates and left the two female wolves' bodies. They'd already consumed the males. They were ready to search for new creatures to kill.

After all, this area was now devoid of prey.

CHAPTER SIX

The large wolf hopped through the hole in the restricted area's fence. Off to the side lay a discarded warning. Great injury and/or death could be incurred through encounters with the animals in the restricted area. Also, any trespassers not killed by the dinosaurs would be prosecuted to the fullest extent of the law (CFR 36 99:1). He sniffed the sign only because one of the raptors had dropped guano there.

Wolf puppies screamed in his head. Their mother howled balefully.

The wolf backed away from the sign, his face darting left and right. The past ballooned in his mind.

These were the same dinosaurs that had murdered his family. He was certain of it. The wolf's golden eyes tightened into narrow slits. He growled into this new world. Forget about forming his own pack with dinosaurs. He had a new goal in mind: kill the raptors.

The wolf howled low and long, a song of redemption for his pack, then he galloped into the white and black mountains, tracking the Utahraptors. He followed them to the edge of one forest where they had killed bison. A couple of bears were picking the bison clean. The wolf had never encountered a bear before. They didn't look near as big or dangerous as an Allosaurus, but he wasn't sure he wanted to approach them, either. He gave them a wide berth.

A better use of his time was studying the scents the raptors left behind. He smelled at the base of trees and then followed his nose upward. He so rarely stared up at tree branches. Up did not provide information. Only birds and pterosaurs remained up. *Smell fell* was the general rule, though he knew scents could float in the breeze and rise on drafts. He liked looking at the intersecting branches.

For the rest of the day, the wolf chased the raptors. As the hours grew long, their smell became difficult to track. He entered a freshly burned forest. The smoke and ash were strong here. It made the raptor's scent harder to detect, but the wolf was undaunted. He knew he was closing in, and the closer he got to them, the more he imagined killing them.

He had a dream that night while he slept under a smoking log. He dreamed he encountered the raptors. It was raining despite the snowfall. Everything was wet, and yet, as the droplets hit the dead forest, the logs sizzled.

The raptors congregated around a kill. The wolf smiled, licking his lips and baring his teeth. Staying low, he crept close to the raptors. Their faces were turned away as the raptors concentrated on the kill in front of them. He was so near, he could practically taste the flesh on their tails. When he pounced, the raptors swiveled. They'd been expecting him. The wolf barked and snapped in a frenzy. Everywhere was raptor teeth and claws, and then they were all on top of him, holding him down with their horrible talons. The large one raked his crescent moon claw over the lone wolf's throat. He was his mother all over again, held down by a large raptor with a burned face.

The wolf fought back. In the struggle, the large raptor sliced his throat open.

And then the wolf woke up, kicking his back feet and darting out from under the smoking log.

It was so early the moon was still a blind eye floating in the sky, but he wouldn't be going back to sleep anytime soon. The wolf picked up the scent where it dipped down through a ravine.

There, he found several large piles of raptor guano. A mark warning all other creatures to keep away from this area. This was raptor territory.

Inside the raptor's marked area, the wolf discovered a different species of animal. He'd seen them occasionally, in mechanical beasts that made lots of noise as they drove around the valley.

This particular creature lay slumped against a tree. It had once stood tall. It had pinkish flesh in parts, and two legs, but it was missing an arm, and it was very dead. Long-time dead. The wolf put his mouth on the young man's flesh and tugged a piece. Something felt wrong to him. Perhaps it was the untouched state of the body, as if all other creatures in the forest, including the birds, had left the human alone because it was marked by the raptors.

The wolf jumped over the body, kicking off the torn "West Lake" shirt, and continued his search. He found two more corpses. The raptors had shoved the bodies into a burned tree. Feet and hands bulged from the hole in positions that defied their biology.

The bodies were not badly decomposed. They were no more than a few weeks old.

The wolf continued his hunt.

Five miles deeper into the mountains, he discovered another section of land comprised of recently burned woods. Here he found two dead raptors. The wolf was taken back by the sight for only a moment. He hadn't seen Utahraptors since he was a pup. They had become a nightmare he'd buried deep in his subconscious. He hadn't thought of the raptors in months. It was only their smell that jolted him back into this life.

One was a little raptor, barely old enough to eat on his own. He was less than half the size of a human. His skin was shriveled and leathery. Somehow, he was smaller than when he was alive. As with the humans, no animal had touched the raptor, as if touching it would bring a curse.

The second raptor lay not far from the first, crushed under a large branch.

These monsters killed his siblings and parents. If he wanted, he could pull them apart and search for any meat under their blackened crust, but eating them seemed to validate their role in the natural order, which some deep part of him knew they weren't a part of.

He hunched over one dead raptor and dropped a giant wolf turd on its body. He kicked his feet behind him as he walked away. *That's for my pack*, his lurid actions proclaimed.

He roamed all afternoon, crossing back to the far side of the restricted area. He encountered no other dinosaurs the rest of the day.

When he slept that night, he dreamed the human corpses had come to life to slay the dinosaurs and the wolf. He retreated into the woods, followed by the vicious raptors. He was mad at the humans for treating him like a dinosaur. The dinosaurs were ashen sticks that ripped him apart.

As he was ripped into pieces, he fell like leaves to the ground, where he became solid again. He was a puppy nursing on his mother's milk. The world was warm and soft, and he was surrounded by his littermates.

He awoke scared and alone. He howled his heart to the moon. The more he remembered his dead family, the more he ached.

The next morning, the wolf did not walk far before encountering another body. An old man had been dragged through the underbrush and up into a tree. The corpse was destroyed more than eaten. The raptors had gone after the meat in the man's thighs and arms but left most of the rest of the body unconsumed and exposed. Again, the wolf did not harvest any food from the corpse.

The wolf wondered how a dinosaur got that high into a tree. Dinosaurs were full of surprises.

He investigated further. There were two more humans. They fled, breaking small tree branches and crushing grass stalks carelessly along their path of retreat. The raptors hunted them for many miles but kept their distance. After tracking the pursuit for half a day, he found pink flesh and a bearded face sticking out of the snow like a discarded and forgotten toy.

He pawed at the snow around the body. Large valleys were ripped into the hunter's legs and torso. He'd fallen on his back and fought the raptors supine. Easily killed, the hunter was also left uneaten, and the raptors hadn't bothered to hide the remains.

As the wolf pushed deeper into the dark forest, he picked up additional smells that told the story of this new animal, these humans. Humans were neither meat eaters nor plant eaters. They consumed anything and everything, vegetables and animals. The stench of their consumption contaminated their tracks, but there was more. Though the wolf did not know the words or concepts of things like grass-fed beef or Gore-Tex boots, he could read the scent left behind by this last hunted human.

This one human remained, pursued by the monsters that had killed the wolf's family. The wolf crossed the mountains to get to them. Unlike the other hunters, this man's odor undulated blue like a wave that was sad, but powerful. Like a man raised by wolves. He didn't reek of gunpowder like the other two men. His scent mixed together pine, metal, string, and leather.

The wolf was close.

The raptors were maybe a hundred yards from him. He loped, then sprinted. His senses grew more attuned to the moment with every step.

And then the wind changed drastically. The branches on the dead trees knocked against the trunks and snapped. The wolf raised his head high into the air. Cooler breezes and a drop in air pressure warned him a storm was coming. His hunt would have to wait. He needed to find shelter or freeze to death. The problem was, where could this giant of a wolf hide? He didn't have his tree stump and roots to crawl into, and the logs here were thin and broken.

Fortunately, large stones jutted out of the snow. They looked like the lower jawbone of Fenrir, his teeth still standing tall after a millennium after his death. The wolf followed only the religion of the trail, and he harbored no interest in culture. But even he was taken back by the image.

The wolf was not "in" or "under" a stone, but he felt safe here, and the stones would provide at least some shielding. If he'd been born with the packs in Yellowstone, he may have slept in the open, unafraid of the world's creatures. But this wolf grew up where giants ruled the mountainside.

The wolf dug into the snowfall between two long, sharp-looking teeth. He tucked his nose into his tail and waited out the violent storm. He thought of the raptors and how good it would feel to break their long necks in his jaws.

He did not sleep. The storm flowed over the mountains and poured over him. The howl of the wind was the ghostly howls of his family and the growls of their killers. He tried to retain the smell of the raptors for as long as possible until the wind and snow buried it. His cruel, golden eyes twinkled, never dimmed by the raging storm. How could a storm compare to the rage of a child whose parents were murdered?

Hours later, when the storm subsided, the wolf pushed out from under the new white snowpack. He shook off his frosted cap and returned to the hunt.

Turning down a draw, the wolf knew he was getting close. The raptors were not far ahead. He picked up his pace. He was so eager, had waited so long, he was almost salivating with his hunger for vengeance. He was becoming the fast, undetected death that comes against the wind. The thief in the night.

And the wolf was in luck. The raptors had trapped the last human like a badger in his hole. Perfect. They were distracted.

He charged into the fury.

PART THREE: SURPLUS KILLERS

The dominant primordial beast was strong in Buck, and under the fierce conditions of trail life it grew and grew. Yet it was a secret growth. His newborn cunning gave him poise and control.
Jack London, The Call of the Wild

If you want to go fast, go alone. If you want to go far, go together.
– African proverb

CHAPTER ONE

"What. The. Hell?" I asked the wolf in front of me. The wolf lay centered in my flashlight beam, licking his paws, which were covered in Utahraptor blood. Two red streaks ran down the wolf's sides.

"They should have ripped you open," I said, taking in his wounds.

The wolf paused to eye me. I swallowed my next words, which were "Oh, shit. Don't look him directly in the eye." I found a spot on the wall to hold my attention. The wolf eventually returned to his paws, but not too quickly. He wanted to remind me who was in charge.

So many thoughts were plowing through my brain, but first and foremost was what I could do to protect myself. I mean, this wolf was HUGE. And it had fought off dinosaurs.

I reached for my arrows. The wolf gave a little growl, a sound my mind equated with olden-time schoolmarms clearing their throats to warn young students that a ruler slap would quickly follow if they didn't desist this instant. And like that student, my hand stopped in midair. I retracted it. Was this wolf going to eat me? Why was he here? What did he want?

"Are you even a he?" I let slip. I usually wasn't this careless, but there was a giant wolf sitting in front of me, and it had *just chased off three Utahraptors.* Cut me some slack.

Head to tail, the wolf was almost two thirds the length of my Chevy Colorado. Put another way, if I lined up my two German Shepherds, Bodak and Mordor, nose to tail, this wolf was longer than their total length combined. The wolf was so long, its paws lay at the back of the trench by me, and its tail rested on the snow outside the front opening. The beast was tall enough to look me in the eye when we stood.

My mind ticked through comparisons. I'd hunted ten-foot tall bears that could shake a stout tree when they rubbed their backs against it, and I'd hunted wolves in Canada that were nine-feet long, but no, nothing compared to this.

"Your Mama must've been a big one," I said.

The wolf ignored my attempt at small talk, which was probably a good thing.

"You're like a dire wolf, or a warg. Warg. I think I'll call you that."

The wolf glanced back at me. Golden eyes shimmered in the darkness.

"Okay, Warg it is. I'm going to reach for my pack now, Warg. I have food in there. I need to eat. I bet you need food, too."

Slowly, my hand stretched to my pack. The wolf stopped and watched my hand. Remember, I was cornered in the back of the wilderness shelter when this happened. There was nowhere for me to go.

My breath tightened, and I began to perspire despite the freezing temperatures. "Are you going to bite my arm off? 'Cause you could." The wolf remained quiet.

A very tense second passed as I slowly pulled the backpack to me. The wolf's eyes followed the pack. I unzipped it. At the sound, the wolf pushed back, a little alarmed.

"It's okay. It's okay," I repeated. I agonized over every loud metal rip of the zipper. When a hole opened in the pack large enough to fit my hand, I was very thankful. The wolf was still tensed up, but he did not react. He studied my every move, though.

I removed a package of venison jerky. The cellophane wrapper crinkled way too loudly in the night.

Please don't eat me. Please don't eat me.

The wolf stood up and watched me carefully. At this point, a few drops of blood dribbled from the wolf's mouth and I realized the wolf didn't have sore paws; he was hungry and licking the raptor's blood.

I fully opened the package and pushed a plug of wet venison into my mouth. I chewed it in a way that would get my butt tossed out of cotillion. I ate that way so that the smell of the venison would roll around in the air and drift to the wolf. It must've worked because Warg extended his nose to my mouth. He licked the side of my mouth. I smiled. It would've been cute and endearing if Warg wasn't a menacing monster covered in the blood of his enemies.

The wolf ripped the extended plug of venison out of my lips. It was gone in a flash down the wolf's maw.

"Good Warg," I said. I put another strip in my mouth. The wolf cocked his head to the side. I kept chewing. Again, the giant wolf licked my mouth, then ripped the plug away.

I didn't know a ton about dogs (my folks weren't really dog people), but I'd seen documentaries. Warg was behaving like a pup, licking the lips of an older wolf who would regurgitate food for him. What was going on in this dog's head?

"You must be hungry, Warg. I don't have enough to feed a thing your size, but maybe we can share. I'm hungry, too."

I shoved a third one in my mouth and chomped it. The wolf licked at my mouth, but the plug had already disappeared behind my lips.

The wolf put his paw on my face. It was a big damn paw. Rough as sandpaper. It scraped the side of my cheeks as he dropped his paw.

"Hey! My turn with the food!" I said.

The wolf stood up on all four legs, and I nearly lost my bowels. Massive shoulders touched the shelter's ceiling. The wolf's nose shot forward. *This is it*, I thought. *I'm dead.*

The wolf pushed me back with his head. It wasn't unlike being pushed by a horse when it shoves you backwards with its head. Stupid me, I pushed back. In movies, this would be the moment where the wolf wagged his tail or rolled over like a dog and we bonded. God, I hoped it worked.

This wasn't a movie. The wolf pushed harder for the food. I got the distinct feeling the wolf was trying to shove his mouth inside mine, so I swallowed fast, then opened wide.

"See. All g-ah!"

I got a mouthful of wolf nose, sniffing around for the venison.

I shoved the wolf away. This time, though, I tossed my last two strips of venison in front of the wolf. "Yours," I said.

In the distance, a raptor screamed. The wolf shot out of the shelter and looked around. Then he ducked his head back into the shelter. "You coming?" the wolf implied with his face.

And what a face it was. Broad and round because of his size, with gray fur and a long, white mouth. A black stripe ran the length of his back, turned gray on his head, and blazed down the wolf's nose. White splotches above his eyebrows highlighted his golden eyes.

The wolf yipped. "Let's go!"

"I'm coming!" I said, throwing on my now-dry clothes and grabbing my gear and my pack. I didn't know who was alpha, or if it even mattered. He'd saved my life, and he was doing a lot better at catching raptors than I'd been.

I followed the wolf into the embattled woods. Clear, dark skies reigned after the passing of the storm. The blizzard, having wiped the slate clean, scrubbed even the tiniest clouds from the sky. The stars like a thousand-eyed monster watched us from above.

But I felt better with the wolf at my side.

CHAPTER TWO

"At my side" isn't entirely accurate. Warg may have been big as a bear, but he moved with the speed of a wolf. I had to run just to stay within viewing distance, which wasn't easy because my leg was still sore from yesterday's crash landing. Occasionally, Warg would stop in the distance and look over his shoulder at me to make sure I was following.

Through icy breaths I grumbled to myself.

"I'm losing my...mind. I've gone crazy. I'm...literally following a wild animal...into the woods. I think we're hunting...dinosaurs, but I'm not sure.... But I'm alive. I'd be dead if not for you, you...glorious wolf. Monster. Warg."

He was there, then he was gone. I picked up speed, keeping one eye on the white-coated ground beneath me and one in the general direction of where I last saw him. I caught up to where I thought he should be, but nothing. I checked the four corners, then cussed.

I'd lost him in the forest.

The possibility that I'd lost him was mindboggling. Everything about Warg was super-sized, including his paws. His paws were so tremendous, I should've tracked him easily through the snow, but Warg was surprisingly light-footed. Where was he?

It took me hours to finally find him again. By then it was dark, and I was starting to suspect I'd imagined him. I just kept running and searching. I was running, and then suddenly I was in a different forest, on a different mountain, and I was covered in blood. I was running back to the road, raising my cellphone to try and get service. My face was so soaked in tears, my skin was raw.

"Come on!" I yelled. "Come on!"

The truck wasn't that far. I could get help. This didn't have to be how it ended. And still, I knew this was exactly how it would end. We don't get a choice in our beginnings or our endings, just the stuff in the middle.

This was the worst moment in my life. The bottom. I was so helpless. I couldn't do anything. I was a complete and total failure. I had just lost everything – everything that made me who I was. I was balling my eyes out and screaming and nothing was working. From this point forward, I would be a God-Damned Thing. Not even human.

Because I was overcome with emotion and trying to get a signal, I didn't see what was right in front of me. I tripped and fell face-first into snow.

And then SLAM! Back with the wolf and the dinosaurs.

I nearly ran over him.

Warg was crouched low. How this giant wolf that could look me in the eye could also sneak so low among the sedge grass was inconceivable, which only added to my growing belief that this was all complete insanity and I must be dreaming. It was a death-dream, and I was back at the shelter being disemboweled by Utahraptors, but in my death dream I was following a giant wolf into the afterlife. Heaven? Hell? Valhalla? Maybe I should ask Warg if he prefers the name Fenrir.

My good leg nearly struck Warg, who side-eyed me, his glare utter exasperation. By Warg's posture, I could tell he was hunting, so I dropped to my belly next to the giant wolf. For a moment, I just soaked in the gigantic size of the animal. The hairs in his gray fur rippled like wheat fields in the wind. The wind was blowing toward us. We were downwind. Damn skippy.

My eyes trailed Warg's. A lone raptor stood in the middle of the dead trees. The one I shot in the hand with my arrow. The arrow was still embedded in his palm like a porcupine quill. He was sniffing his wound and walking in circles.

Warg and I shared a look. Oh, this was a bait trap.

I whispered to him, "They're baiting us, but where are the other two?"

They might be using a blind. Okay, not a camouflage tarp, but a blind all the same. The trick was to find it. I remembered when they hunted me, how they stayed in my periphery. I checked to my left and to my right, but I saw neither hide nor claw of the Utahraptors, and there just wasn't any coverage unless they'd suddenly discovered the ability to reduce their width to hide behind sticks and trees.

"I say I take the shot. I know the other two are out there somewhere, but if I kill this raptor, they lose the numbers game. We're two-v-two. Right?"

Warg's face was emotionless.

"I'll take that as a yes."

I notched a broadhead with a special glow notch so that I didn't lose it in the darkness. I adjusted my sight to twenty yards. The little neon green pin put a dot on the raptor's spine. I was close enough to kill. If the raptor would shift his head ever so slightly more perpendicular to me, that would be a big help. I could hit the heart and get a clean kill.

Even after all I'd been through, and as dangerous as I knew these predators were, I still preferred a clean kill. Sure, I didn't want the animal to suffer more than it had to. But if I'm being honest, I just wanted to kill the bastard that had been chasing me for the past two days.

The raptor's head drew left. I held my breath. I drew back on the bowstring. This always brought me closer to the kill. It sounds strange, but it tunes me in. The background blurs around me as the details of my quarry suddenly illuminate in high definition. I saw a broken neck spine, nicked flesh, and faded scars. As I drew back, the world fell away and the arrow's plastic featherings gently caressed my cheek. A lover's touch. *Turn*, I willed the raptor. *Tuuuuuurn*.

Warg growled first. Then a sound like electric mayhem exploded overhead. I glanced up in time to see the two remaining raptors dropping down from the trees like Navy SEALs. Warg rose to meet them, jaws open. The raptors collided with the wolf. They clamped their arms on his shoulders, bit down, and flicked their nasty feet claws at his belly.

Seeing the attack was a thing of startling beauty. Dangerous, yes, but beautiful, too. The raptors ripped at Warg with those wicked sabers that were shaped like horned moons. Each talon was over a foot long and, at their thickest, they were as big around as my arm. I remembered how vividly Mad Dog described Jonah's cut. Seeing the talons from this close, I was dumbfounded by awe and terror. There was this moment when I realized how insignificant man's weapons are next to an animal's.

In five seconds, I'd been completely dethroned from my place atop the food chain, and I didn't like where I sat. For the first time, I understood why early humans killed off all the giant prehistoric animals, the saber-tooths and the mammoths and the dire wolves. The idea of living in a world bountiful with such horrors was just too scary, and they needed to be eliminated. All of them.

Warg shoved Jonah and the other raptor down on the ground. He landed on them with a thud. Men's spines would have been shattered, but these raptors were built of sturdier stuff than mere mortals.

The raptors bit down on his ankles. Warg barked and snapped. The raptors shook, and he jumped off them. Now they were circling each other.

At this point, the mix of awe and terror released me, and I suddenly remembered the third Utahraptor. I turned in time to meet the gaze of the raptor as it rushed me. Adrenaline surging, everything slowed down in that moment. Mid-pivot, two long arms reached around me. My body kept spinning. The raptor's face emerged from the darkness. My neon green pin lined up with its eye. The arrow released. Raptor collided with human, and the world turned upside down several times, suddenly in fast forward.

I blanked out. I wasn't sure what exactly happened, but isn't that how it goes with near-death experiences? And I'd never had a near-death experience as scary as that one. Yes, I'd killed many large predators, but they never got so close to me. That was the point of hunting. You sat and you waited until the animal got within range to kill, and then you released the arrow immediately. You don't wait until it's almost on top of you.

Fortunately, I'd only blanked out for a few seconds. Unfortunately, that meant I was brought back into a world of screaming and snarling. Blood splashed on my face, and I don't know to whom it belonged.

The raptor with my arrow in the side of his face stopped to push it out. Quickly I grabbed another neon-notch arrow and fired. Got him!

The raptors were retreating, and as they disappeared into the night, I could follow the little glowing notch sticking out of the raptor's calf.

Or not. I don't know if you're familiar with light-up arrows. Once they hit their mark and the animal scurries away, it's up to you to follow the little bright light. The good news is, it's easy to locate a neon light in the middle of an unlit wilderness. The bad news is, that little bouncing light flew as soon as the dinosaur took off. It arced up and down, up and down fast as a deer.

I bolted after the shot raptor. No thinking, no fear. My eyes didn't check the ground for the black tips of rocks or the mound bulges belying hidden dangers under snowfall. Everything that wasn't that little green light faded away.

Here's the thing about chasing deer. When it's a good shot, after about thirty yards or so, most deer slow down. This wasn't a good shot, but still, what I saw defied logic. The raptor sped up. The little light receded farther and farther from me, no matter how fast I sprinted. Catching it was hopeless.

I stopped to heave air into my tired lungs. I made big wheezing sounds in the dry California winter. As I heaved, my eyes never left that light. It kept going and going and going…

And then the light darted up a tall tree and vanished.

Again, this never happened with anything else I'd hunted. Up? The tree?

The raptors were gone. They'd merged with what a poet once called "the caliginosity of the void."

CHAPTER THREE

I returned to Warg, who was still back where we'd fought the raptors. Warg lay on his side out of view. I honestly worried the great wolf was maimed. I circled around to the wolf's side, tense as my bowstring when an arrow is drawn. Dying predators were as dangerous as they come.

Warg was playing with one of my $50 arrows. A couple must have spilled out of my quiver when I ran after the raptors. He mouthed my expensive hunting equipment like a chew toy, swiveling his head around.

His eyes shined in the darkness.

Despite the damage, I laughed. I had no stinking clue what was going on. Raptors can climb trees and run faster than deer. And this giant wolf was playing with my arrows.

"Yep. I've definitely lost my mind."

Warg shot up immediately, surprised. He snapped the carbon arrow in his teeth. Like a toothpick.

"Hey! That costs good money."

He growled a little warning about the policies of wolf economics. It reminded me of his schoolmarm growl in the back of the shelter. I took a measured step back.

"I shot the raptor with a glow arrow," I said, getting either him or me up to speed. "It didn't do jack for me. They all ran away. Thanks for the assist, by the way."

I pointed as I explained. Warg's gaze followed my line of direction. He dropped the arrow and leaped to his feet, then took off into the woods like he understood exactly what I'd said.

"Wait!" I called after him.

The wolf stopped.

"I-I can't. I'm tired. I've been running for like, forever. I want to get them, too, but I'm very hungry and I need to rest." I rubbed my belly as if wolves grasp sign language.

The wolf cocked his head. The utter lack of emotion in the wolf's face was scarier than anything I'd seen that day. The face could be tallying the numerous ways to kill me and deliberating which was the best choice, or it could be considering cuddling with me. It was so completely blank, I had no idea.

So I restated, "Hungry." I moved an invisible spoon to my mouth several times, even though there was again no reason for a wolf to understand what that meant. I lay my head on an imaginary pillow knowing full well that wolves did not sleep in beds and did not fluff their pillows. "Tired."

The wolf licked his mouth.

I sat down and hung my head. "I'm talking to a wolf like he understands English." I wiped my brow and looked up. The wolf was gone.

"And now I'm talking to myself."

I didn't have my sleeping bag or my tent. I did have my magnesium fire starter kit, so I built a small fire and emptied what was left of my pack. No pot to melt ice, but I did have a special foldaway cup that doubled as a pot. I'd vowed to never test its heat durability in a backwoods situation, but I needed to drink. I scooped some snow into the cup and lay down on my empty pack. I scrunched my spare clothes into a bundle and used them as a pillow.

When I woke, the water was steaming hot. The cup hadn't deformed, but how hot was it?

"Ouch!" I cried out when I touched the cup. I used sticks to move the water closer to me. I packed snow around the base to cool it down. I even dropped a small handful of fresh snow into the water.

Then I found a tree. I peed for at least a minute. My urine came out dark, and it steamed on the frozen ground. I didn't poop. I wasn't alarmed by the fact that I hadn't pooped in two days or that my urine was darker than normal. My body was running on reserves I didn't have while burning calories like an Olympic swimmer.

Walking back to camp, about forty yards in front of me, something very large was rummaging in the woods. What was Warg up to?

Warg shuffled backwards, nearly stepping onto the fire. With a twist of his head, he flopped a dead elk down in front of me.

I laughed. "Do you know how many hunters would kill to bring down an elk like that? That head is the envy of every rifleman on the west coast."

Warg's lips pulled back in a big wolfish grin. Hindsight being 20/20, I don't know if he grinned because it was the first praise he'd ever received, or if he was laughing at me because he was used to bringing down much larger and more dangerous prey. Elk was probably nothing for a dinosaur hunter like him. But at that point, I didn't know he was born and raised in the restricted area.

"Good boy," I said. "Good boy, Warg."

His expressive eyebrows scrunched and gave me a weird look, like he didn't know what to do with that. Was I complimenting him or threatening him or just being weird? I could tell he was coming around to me. And it was obvious he understood the gist of me. He knew I was hungry, and I doubt it was 'cause he read sign language.

We were beginning a relationship, but where this relationship was going, I don't think either of us truly knew.

How long ago was it when humans and wolves first came together to hunt? This was perhaps the first time in fifteen thousand years that wolves and humans had hunted together. Evolution was cyclical. I wondered if the relationship that created dogs had come full circle to me and this wolf hunting dinosaurs. If this was the kind of situation that forged the first bonds between humans and canines, what did that mean for our hunt? Was everything coming back to this? Or maybe Warg and I were forging new relationships that would redefine the bond between animal and human?

I went to work preparing the kill using the gut hook knife. I split the elk's hide, removed the organs, and tossed them to Warg. He gulped them down greedily. The buck was more than I could eat in a month, and there was no way I was getting the head back to the truck (much as I would have liked), so I decided against preparing the elk for consumption and taxidermy. Instead, I removed enough meat for myself, and I cooked it on a makeshift spit I erected over the fire. Warg ate the rest.

While the elk meat cooked, I drained every last drop from my cup, then refilled it with fresh snow. I needed to keep hydrated. I sat by the fire and watched Warg munch on the elk's carcass. It was afternoon, and the winter sun was setting. I pinched myself one more time just to be sure. Nope. I wasn't dead. This was all real.

But just for proof (if I ever survived this crazy stunt), I pulled out my camera phone. When Warg wasn't looking, I snapped a couple photos of him licking the elk's head. What a sight! The buck's long antlers pressed against the sides of Warg's face.

I checked my reception. Still no signal, so the photo was stored locally rather than in a cloud somewhere. I'd feel better if it was stored in a server farm in some city, but then again, if I had a signal, I'd call the sheriff and ask for reinforcements. Hell, I'd ask for an airlift.

As the meat got close to ready, Warg sniffed its savory temptation in the air.

"I've never cooked elk. Not cooked over a campfire like this," I said. "Damn, but that smells good."

I reached down for the gut hook knife. When I looked back up, the stick was gone. The wolf held it between his paws. He shredded the meat with his fangs, ripping off strips of meat.

"Hey!" I stood up. My voice was angry. That elk smelled good.

Warg eyed me.

"That's mine!" I marched over and reached for the meat.

Warg snapped at my face. God, the wind coming from the wolf's quick head movement. It was a blink and his face was in mine, challenging me.

"Okay, fine. Yours. But the next one's mine." I tried to sound as grizzled as possible as I pointed to my chest.

So I cooked another piece on a new stick. Warg had returned to his elk head. Again, as I got close to done, Warg took notice.

"My food, Warg. Back off." Warg stood up and walked over to me. I was squatting down in the snow next to the fire. The wolf towered over me. Didn't make a noise.

I ignored him, though I was terribly unnerved. I kept cooking. The wolf's head lowered until it was on top of me. Warg's breath was warm and humid.

I grimaced.

Defiantly, I ripped a piece off the cooked meat.

Warg roared. He shoved me down, knocking my butt backward. Then he lunged at my neck. I didn't scream, but I didn't push away either. I mean, what could I do? I'd fallen in such a way that my neck was exposed. If this wolf wanted, I was a dead man.

"Go ahead. Kill me. At least then I'll be back with my daughter." I huffed in my chest as we stared at each other, two scarred souls not yet shuffled off this mortal coil.

But Warg didn't kill me. He snapped and flashed his fangs over my neck. His hot drool dripped and drained over my cheek. I didn't move. Just kept staring at him angrily. I wasn't going to back down in this. Warg backed off. He grabbed my meat from the fire and consumed it like he stole it and expected me to get it back. When he looked back, I hadn't moved. I glowered. He walked away.

I cooked one more piece of meat. This time, Warg left me alone. Whenever I glanced over at him, he looked at me all sweet and innocent. Who could believe that sweet angel could kill? Ha! You can't fool me.

The meat tasted excellent, by the way. Everybody should have to fight a wolf for their meal. It'd teach them to value the food on their table.

I drank deeply and often, peed again, and finished my meal. Warg lay next to the elk's half-eaten body, soaking up the fire's warm glow.

"You are one scary mystery," I said. The wolf's eyes seemed to say as much back to me. Introductions were needed.

"Me? I'm Cody. Cody Morris. Thanks for asking. I'm a hunter. Actually, I have a day job, but it's not important to knowing who I am. My life as a hunter defines me. I've hunted all my life. But these past few years have been real hard."

The wolf watched me with that blank face. There was no judgement in his golden eyes.

"Good question," I said, shaking the darkness from my soul. "I don't think I've told you about my daughter. Don't be offended."

Swear to God, the wolf looked mildly offended.

I said, "I don't tell people about her. A few years ago, I brought my daughter out for her first hunt. Isabelle. I called her Izzy. I was going to show her how to bow hunt. It was going to be special. She didn't know that. She wasn't really into hunting, but neither was I when I was her age. She wanted to play video games and text her friends. After telling her to put away the cellphone about a dozen times, I finally had to take it. I jerked it out of her hands, and I shoved it in the glove compartment and locked it. She was so mad at me. I mean, I think you know what anger is, but those raptors have nothing on a pre-teen."

"I decided to make it up to her. Once we stopped the car and while we unloaded our gear, I showed her the new compound bow I bought for her. I spent a lot of money on this bow. You've got to understand, these things aren't cheap to begin with. I worked overtime, you know?"

"She'd shot before, but she'd never owned her own bow. I'd had it especially made for her. Bright pink outline over a camouflage inlay. Pink was her favorite color. I had to pay extra for that. And when I showed it to her, I did it like I was presenting her an Oscar. I was so excited to finally give her the bow."

"You wouldn't understand this because you're a wolf, but Izzy wasn't impressed. She was about as far from impressed as she could get, and she sure showed it. She scoffed and looked away. I passed it off like it was no big deal, even though I was tearing up inside. We hiked out when we arrived. Like all fathers, I tried to build the hunt up. I knew I'd upset her earlier, and I didn't want that to linger. It could stink up the whole hunt, and this was a special one. I think it is with wolves, too. The first hunt? It matters."

"So I told Izzy about hunting and camping and how important it is because we are all energy and hunting is about energy flowing from the string to the deer, and even though that energy consumes a life, it continues through us when we eat the deer. The energy we put into the world comes back to us. The energy continues life."

"She told me that hunting was an outdated concept fueled by Republican propaganda and that the act of hunting constituted cruel and unusual punishment. I tell you, there is no fervor like the fire of youth. And it wasn't just hunting that she was so opinionated about. Izzy felt so passionately about everything. She thought I was this horrible person who stood for everything wrong in the world. I beamed with pride. I truly enjoyed every conversation. If I'd known what was happening next, I would have memorized every word of our arguments. I'd have taped it, recorded it. Something. They say love is a dying ember, and it's true. No matter how permanent I try to make the memories, they fade away."

I poked the fire a bit. "Izzy watched me as we checked her arrows and her bow. Inspected the feathering, the balance, the weight. You have to know the feel of your arrows. When hunting with a rifle, nobody'd think of handling the bullets. But bowhunting is different. It's more personal. Everybody thinks it's William Tell seeing so perfectly the apple on his son's head, but it's as much about touch as it is about visualization. So she practiced checking her arrows. I could see that the ritual was changing her the way it had changed me, too, when my father taught it to me."

"I reviewed the safety rules that night. Always wear hunter orange. I know I don't now, but things have changed. It was important back then. I told Izzy to be sure of her target, in front of and behind. Never point an arrow at anything you don't intend to shoot. Things like that. When we were done, I grilled tofurkey (her request) and we went to sleep."

"Early the next morning, we set out. I found a good place to wait for the deer. We didn't have to wait long. The most beautiful, biggest stag you've ever seen appeared to her. A Rocky Mountain Mule Deer. At first, she was taken by its beauty. *Izzy*, I prodded. *It's time.*"

"*Are you sure I should be doing this?*"

"*Trust me*, I said."

"Izzy pulled the bowstring back to her cheek, took a deep breath, and released. The arrow flew straight and pure. The stag leaped at the last second and ran into the forest."

"*Come on! Let's go*. I encouraged her. We pursued the stag. It was so fast. As it ran, it wiggled its tail at us. It jumped from side to side. What made it really peculiar was that the stag would stop and look over its shoulder at us, as if we were playing an elaborate game of tag."

"My daughter smiled so big. I hadn't seen her smile like that in years. Not since her Mom died. When she retrieved her first arrow, she grinned at me. We had a real connection for the first time in a year. That grin meant everything to me. Even after all these years, I still remember the way it arched back against her face and how her eyes sparkled with joy."

"We chased the stag all over the forest. Down in little gullies, up onto a plateau. We ran and shot, ran and shot. Anytime we got close enough to the stag, she took a shot."

"Finally, we came up close on the stag. Close enough for a kill shot. I handed her an arrow. She pulled it back to her cheek. *Trust yourself*, I said. *Feel the energy*. She took her deep breath, and I took my deep breath. And then. Then I heard an explosion. We both jumped. A hunter behind us hadn't checked in front of his target. We were in the bushes between him and the stag. She hadn't jumped. She'd been knocked over by the shot in her head. In an instant, my beautiful daughter was dead."

I poked the fire some more. I took a deep breath and exhaled all blubbery. "I've never forgiven myself for what happened to Izzy that day."

I tossed the stick into the fire and stood up. Warg watched me with that vacant stare. Tears cut running brooks down my face.

I said, "Look at me, pouring out my heart to a wolf. You know these woods are famous for people going in here and losing their heads? Calavera River is where an ossuary roundhouse was discovered, and Brideshead Mountain is named after a literal bride's head. The woman was decapitated by a jealous woman who cut off her head on her wedding day and brought it up to the mountain. And just like them, I'm losing my head. I'm talking to a wolf, and we're chasing dinosaurs."

Warg laid, paws crossed. Most of the elk head had vanished down his throat. He yawned.

"That's probably the best reaction I could have expected," I said, a small tremble in my voice. The blood soaking the fur around the wolf's mouth was unsettling. "I'll make a deal with you, Warg. You don't kill me, I won't kill you. I'm still not sure why you're hunting raptors, but I believe – No, I *know* – *we* can kill them if we work together. So, what do you say? Partners?"

Warg stood and stretched his hind legs.

"I'll take that as a yes. I think this is going to work. It makes no sense, but when your child is taken from you, nothing makes sense anymore. The real question is how do we communicate? You don't speak a word of English, and I don't know how to talk wolf-speak."

Warg's nose suddenly shot up like he'd caught wind of another elk. A twinkle in Warg's eye told me it wasn't an elk. I remember seeing the same twinkle in my daughter's eyes when she was hunting. I grabbed the compound bow and arrows and tossed my backpack over my shoulders. I had a hard-shell quiver connected to my pack. A simple flick of fabric and a tie-off revealed the full quiver.

Warg ran into the forest.

"Come on Don Quixote," I said. "Let's go tilt at some windmills."

CHAPTER FOUR

In his short life, the wolf had encountered more dangerous and exotic species than most creatures on the planet. Unfortunately, all that experience and history was rendered useless when it came to humans, which the wolf had never encountered before. As a new species, the wolf felt a need to figure out the taxonomy of humans.

Humans were fur-and-flesh animals, like him. Not a scaly or feathered dinosaur. Humans stood on two legs like an Allosaurus or Tyrannosaurus Rex, and those two-legged monsters were always lethal. But this two-legged was different than an Allosaurus. First, his feet lacked claws. They ended in stubby hooves. Second, he showed no capacity for unencumbered ferocity. There was something risky about a human, yes, but at the same time, the wolf kept asking himself, *were they all this stupid?*

Perhaps they are prey. After all, when he first met the human, the man was trapped in a narrow, wooden den while the raptors forced their way inside. As far as the wolf could tell, the human had no other way out of his burrow. No escape route.

Raptors hunt humans. Then again, raptors hunt everything, so perhaps humans were prey to only dinosaurs. The lone wolf was confused. Humans were complicated.

The wolf was an opportunistic predator. While the raptors were distracted by the human in the narrow den, the wolf charged them. He jumped on the back of one, and the raptor rolled him. Raptors fought so meanly. The large wolf and the raptors went back and forth attacking each other, and then one of the raptors cried out in pain. A stick had flown through the air and entered a raptor's claw. When the wolf turned, he was surprised to learn that the human was responsible for the raptor's pain.

Perhaps humans weren't prey after all. Then he had a thought that made him do a mental double-take. Could this human be the pack he'd been searching for? He sat in the human's den and observed him while he tried to make up his mind. The human offered him food.

WHAT?

Nobody had offered him food since his family died! What did this mean? He approached the human as if he were a pup. This was how all his littermates encouraged giving up food. It worked! The venison was delicious.

Suddenly, this human was even more perplexing.

He needed to test him. So when the raptors fled, the wolf chased them. The human ran, too, but the wolf was too fast for the human. His two legs were no match for the wolf's four. The wolf kept having to wait on him. Was this strange? No. The wolf could outrun any animal. Why should a human be any different?

Wolf and human finally caught up to the raptors. The human nearly tripped over him. He was so clumsy compared to a wolf, and he was loud, too. If they were to become a pack, the wolf would have to teach the human to run quietly and observantly. The human crouched down next to him and watched the injured raptor.

Stupid human. Why was he watching the raptor? Did he not smell the raptors in the trees?

Again, the human and his flying arrow helped. They survived the ambush. It was time to run again, but the human couldn't continue. He needed sleep and food. That was obvious. The wolf had seen many starving, exhausted animals before. He considered eating this human, but the strange creature wasn't trying to kill him. He wasn't sure he trusted the human, but the man didn't act like any dinosaur he'd ever met. Maybe there was something to the pack, after all.

Perhaps, the wolf thought, this person was a human pup. Yes, that is it. He's a pup. That explained his ignorance and his fragility.

A pack was only as strong as its pups, so the wolf licked the human pup's face to let him know he was going to get him food. Then he brought down an elk (not easy to do as a lone wolf, but the elk was old). The wolf returned to the human pup with food, like his own father and older siblings used to do. He had considered eating the elk and feeding the human his regurgitation, but the human was unsure of the licking, so he didn't give him any.

When the wolf returned with the kill, he discovered the human had made fire. He'd witnessed fire in the wilderness. He didn't fear fire. He'd seen it damage trees and other animals. This whole side of the mountain stunk of September fire. But that didn't mean it was necessarily bad. Just that it was bad to lesser animals.

Fire was harmful, though. Any creature that could make fire had to be respected, or at least distrusted. Even if that animal was a pup.

The human pup cooked the elk meat. Cooked elk smelled so much better than raw elk! The wolf claimed the first morsel. The human pup seemed angry. This made no sense. There was plenty of meat to go around.

The human cooked more of the elk meat. Well, the first round of elk meat tasted so divine, he was going to eat some more. It was his right as the adult in the pack, after all. When the human pup tried to stop him, he had to put him in his place. It took several times for the pup to learn not to take first food. This pup was stubborn. Or stupid. Or maybe it was just his human-ness.

Whatever the reason, when the wolf finished his meal, he left the carcass for the pup to consume any way he wanted. This was second meat. The pup could have all the second meat he wanted, and he did.

The wolf liked that whole "cooked meat" thing. It smelled better and tasted better. He lay in the snow and dined on the remembered scent. It was so delicious. Should he claim one last piece of meat? He decided not to.

Then the human began making noises with his mouth. He jabbered nonsensically forever and would not shut up. The only other creatures so devoted to chatter were birds. So was this fire-making creature also like a bird?

The human kept looking at him and vocalizing. The wolf didn't know what the sounds meant, but he was not a stupid wolf. "Warg" was human-speak denoting him. He wasn't sure why the human needed to give him a name. He'd never needed a name. What was the point of one? Four little sounds combined into a word failed to tell his whole story. His smell told a much richer and more thorough recounting of who he was. If the human pup wanted to know more about "Warg," he should smell his withers and his rump.

Warg walked beside him to offer his story. The human shut up and froze. He didn't budge his nose any closer to the wolf. The human seemed distressed. What a dunderhead.

Another thing that mystified the wolf was how the human liked to make motions with his front claws. Humans, he decided, had sacrificed speed for gestures, so there must be an important reason for them, but the wolf hadn't figured it out. This would all be easier if the human would start talking like a wolf.

Then the smell came back to him. The stink of murder and sin. The human noticed his wolf nose up in the air. A locking of eyes confirmed that the human knew it was raptors, too, even if he couldn't smell them. The wolf gave chase. The human grabbed his equipment and joined the hunt.

He trotted along a dry riverbed that led up into the mountains. The human fell far behind, so he paused several times when the snow grew deep or the rocks became slick. To try to get the human to hurry faster, he would bark encouragement or whine about the possibility of losing them. He wasn't sure the stupid human pup grasped his meaning.

The scent remained close to the ground, meaning the raptors weren't in the blackened trees. As he ran, the wind in the riverbed would shift. He would have to pause to reassess. If the dinosaurs had moved to a different side of the mountain, the wolf would be able to tell that based on the wind current. He re-sampled the air. They hadn't moved. The raptors were running. Perhaps that was why the shifting air was so confusing.

The wolf jogged up the side of the snow-covered mountain, careful to stay downwind of the dinosaurs. The air here was tighter. It whined and whistled. It was also dry, which meant that it carried very little scent. He had been lucky to discover anything at all. There was a new scent in the air, too. Another human.

He looked back to the hunter human. The pup hadn't noticed the new smell.

The wolf jumped onto a small tor and waited while the hunter struggled to climb up beside him on the rocks. Impatient, the wolf gently lifted the human pup by his scruff and put him on the exposed granite. The human fought him at first, but after the wolf finished moving him, the pup sat on the ledge with his mouth open. The wolf urged him on, but the human didn't move. Had he killed it? The bite wasn't lethal. Perhaps humans were much more fragile than he first believed. They were certainly more stubborn. He had to bark to get the human to stand and walk.

The wolf crossed the top of the tor with slow ease. They were closing in on the raptors. He needed quiet to persevere.

The human was anything but quiet. His clothing grinded against the stone. Was he intentionally trying to alert the dinosaurs to their presence? The human walked beside the wolf, staying low to the ground. The wolf stopped to smell the air. The sulfurous wind had shifted again.

The human raised a black object up to his eyes. The object looked like a rock extending from his face. The wolf did not care what it was. He assumed the object was like any other non-living object and useless.

The human might as well have put a branch up to his head. It would make about as much sense.

If the wolf could have shaken his head or rolled his eyes, he would have. But he was a killer, not a cynic.

"Hunters live and die by the glass." To the wolf, this meant nothing. He wished the human could shut up.

The pair crept further along the outcropping of granite. Falling snow and ice was filling the gaps in the rock and slowly, eon by eon, breaking the rock apart. The wolf could practically smell inevitability wedging into the seams. Beneath them lay long layers of jointed ledges formed by exposed strata.

Suddenly, the sounds of hoofs and claws echoed in Warg's ear drums. He jumped off the tor and shot forward. He had them!

A human was riding a horse through the mountains. The raptors were close behind. The wormy raptor leaped at the rider, bringing certain death. The wolf collided into the raptor mid-air, and they both crashed to the ground. The raptor hissed a warning as it rejoined the chase.

Horse and rider veered toward the ledge. As they ran, rock chips were knocked off the side of the mountain. Jonah put all his weight into his back legs and vaulted up. His athletic body landed on the horse's back. Without hesitation, Jonah bit down on the rider's head. Blood sprayed from her head. The rider screamed as her back arched backward.

The wolf seized the opportunity to take out the burned-face raptor. He'd decided this raptor was the leader of their pack. If he killed him, hunting the others would be easier. He attacked, fangs bared and claws out.

Inexplicably, Jonah let go of the rider and jumped off. Instead of hitting Jonah, the wolf thudded into the back of the horse, nearly knocking it over. Jonah propelled himself off the wolf's back, which the dinosaur hadn't been expecting but was happy to use as his steppingstone. Once on the ground, Jonah continued his pursuit.

These raptors were close to killing the human and her horse.

An arrow glanced off Jonah's burned face. Startled, Jonah barked at the other raptors. They flocked and fled down the side of the mountain as adeptly as native mountain goats. It was an acrobatic angle of descent that even the wolf could not follow.

CHAPTER FIVE

Oh, she's dead. At least, that's what I thought. Those raptors had worked a number on her. Not only was her body crisscrossed with rips, but a piece of her skull was flapping in the wind. I'm no doctor, but I've killed lots of things and seen death way too often, and skull flapping seems like the qualification of dead.

So I was astounded when the woman opened her eyes. Her bright black eyes followed me as I approached her in the saddle. She was ethnic. I don't mean that in a derogatory way. I mean that because I never got to learn her ethnicity. Some type of Asian/Hispanic/Indigenous. Her heart-shaped, olive-complexion face had turned ashen. "You're one of the hunters, aren't you?" she asked weakly.

"Cody Morris."

"The bowhunter?" The inherent gravity of her words and the forlorn look in her eyes told me so many things. First, that she knew of our hunting party, and I didn't think Sheriff Castillo to be the type of person to tell many people about what me, Jan, and Mad Dog were doing in the Perdidos Mountains. So either news got out, or this woman was in his trusted circle. Since the mountains weren't swarming with helicopters and a few hundred hunters, I assumed the latter. The second thing her look told me was that in her mind, if the other hunters were dead, all was lost. She was a coach without a starting quarterback on fourth down with ten seconds left in the game. I was a little insulted, but I'd never considered myself much of a Hail Mary pass any way.

"You need help," I said.

"I need a surgeon and a medical team. That's not going to happen. Help me down."

I walked around her bay-and-white Paint Horse and helped her maneuver her boot out of the stirrup. Then I helped her off. As she leaned into me, a slender line of blood dripped from her leathers to my Patagonia jacket. Once down, her body collapsed. I pulled her weight into me and dragged her away from the Paint. Blood oozed from the back of her head. Warg watched her warily. He didn't want to stop the chase for anyone.

"That's a big damn wolf," the woman exclaimed, her eyes widening with fear and admiration. "I mean, really damn big."

"I know. We're hunting the raptors."

"Together?" Her voice was more than a little alarmed.

I nodded. I helped her to sit under a tall Ponderosa. She groaned as she leaned back.

"You need to rest."

"I was hunting the raptors. I didn't do so well. They got my rifle."

"They killed Jan and Mad Dog, too."

She closed her eyes for a moment before opening them again. "I need to tell you something. You need to be careful with these raptors. They're deviously intelligent. Extremely dangerous."

I fed her the line from my Camelbak. "I know."

She took the bite valve in her mouth and drank thirstily. When she was finished, she said, "You don't understand. I worked for GD Pharma, one of the companies biomanufacturing those monsters. We tampered with the genetic material. Their genomes, their neurology, their chemistry. These creatures are biological machines made to churn out cures to cancer and heart disease. This didn't always happen. Raptors were more different than anything else. They kill anything and everything they come into contact with. They're relentless killing machines."

"I've hunted killing machines before."

She took a deep breath and said, "Lions and tiger and bears, oh my, right? You're still thinking like a 20th century man. They're a plague, Mr. Morris. They must not be allowed to escape the restricted area, and they must not be allowed to reproduce. That would be catastrophic."

"I'm not here to watch them, ma'am. I plan to kill them."

"All of them. I told my superiors, but all they see is the fallout if anybody discovers the truth about these creatures. They made me sign an NDA that I wouldn't talk. So it's up to you to kill them all. If you don't, hundreds, if not thousands of people could die before the raptors are destroyed."

She looked at Warg. "And that wolf, somehow he's part of it."

"Warg is just a wolf."

She shook her head.

"I've heard strange stories of the non-dinosaurs living in the restricted area. They've evolved in ways we cannot fathom. Have you heard of punctuated evolution?" When I said no, she took a deep breath and said, "That's okay. Think 'rapid evolution.' Rapid evolution is happening everywhere inside the park and on the outskirts. The animals are evolving to meet the challenge of Big Pharma's dinosaurs. With everything I've told you about the dinosaurs, can you see why this evolutionary spike must not be allowed to carry on? It's not just about the dinosaurs, but the animals, too."

She removed a pistol from inside her leather fringed jacket. It was an old-fashioned Colt revolver, a gift passed down the family line, I was sure of it. I was so busy studying the pistol, I didn't consider why she'd pulled the gun. She fired it at Warg. I pushed up on her arm as the gunfire ricocheted through the mountains.

Warg jumped. The bullet grazed the trees beside him. His legs stiffened.

"You can't kill Warg! I need him to help me take down the raptors."

Her eyes were droopy, but she was indignant. "That is not a wolf. That is an abomination. It needs to be put down before it can do more damage."

She tried to shoot him again. I shoved her hand aside. Two more shots went off. Warg ran in circles, confused and scared.

"No!" I growled. I slammed her arm into the tree. She gave it up easily.

"What's wrong with you?" She grunted, but she was too weak to stop me.

"We hunt together. You wouldn't understand."

She took a deep breath. She spoke in short sentences to conserve her energy. "You're right. I don't understand. But you're going to have to get right with this, Mr. Morris. This is all on you."

"I know."

"I need to sleep."

Her head slumped to the side. Blood streamed out of her dark hair and stained the snow where she sat. For a moment, I didn't know what to do. Should I bury her? How would I bury her on to of a granite mountain?

I set her down on a limestone slab and covered her body with stones and rocks. I set a waypoint so that her body could be retrieved later, assuming I ever get location services again. And assuming I survived this.

I checked the pistol. Empty. I quickly rummaged through her saddle bags and soon found a box full of extra bullets, but when I opened it and turned it over in my palm, nothing fell out. I was so angry, I could have ripped all the branches out of the tree and torn them into a million pieces. I chunked the box of empty bullets first, and when that didn't satisfy my frustration, I tossed the pistol into the snow.

Warg sat behind a tree, alarm dancing over his face. He'd probably never heard a gunshot before in his life.

Many people try to say that different things separate humans from animals. Environmentalists, nature lovers, animal wardens all want to know why animals fear humans. I can't speak for the last couple of eons, but today, the sound of gunfire gives man dominion over the animals. It will send any creature running. Let me tell you, the bear that doesn't run from gunfire has mental deficiencies.

I approached Warg slowly. He was hunkered low, his tail between his legs. I imagine the woman's gunfire scared him half to death. I moved slowly.

He whined.

"I know. It's okay, boy. It's going to be alright."

His golden eyes were round with fear.

"Don't worry."

When I got close, I extended my hand for him to sniff.

He sniffed the palm of my hand. He pushed his large head into the palm of my hand. I breathed slow and steady.

"One more to avenge, Warg."

CHAPTER SIX

The wolf paced in the snowpack. Hunting raptors was a complicated affair made only more problematic by human interference. The new human's gunshots were an extremely loud tidal wave to his senses. The explosion in the air was magnified in his head. He did not want to encounter that sound ever again in his life.

And then there was the human pup. Once again the wolf's perception of the human was turned upside down. The pup comforted him when he was scared of the gunfire. Not since he was a pup himself had he been comforted by another animal. The wolf needed to explore this nascent feeling that left him confused. Did he trust the hunter?

The human called to the Paint Horse, and the beast of burden came to him quickly. Like the wolf, the horse was all kinds of nervous. The wolf smelled the fear on him. Normally this fear excited him, but now he did not know what to think.

As the wolf approached, the horse neighed and reared up. The human coaxed the horse with his voice. The wolf stayed away. They needed to hurry if they were going to catch up to the raptors.

The dead body, too, the wolf wanted to inspect, but he decided it best to keep his distance. Besides, he could read the rider's story in her smell. She worked with many strange chemicals, she was childless, and she was also a hunter. She'd lived alone except for her horses and her dogs. There was something else in her olfactory profile. Although his vocabulary had no word for it, he smelled the sickness in her. She was stage 4 breast cancer.

The human searched the dead woman, gathered a few items, then covered her in rocks and said a few words to the body. The human wasted way too much time for this. Eventually, finally, he climbed up on the horse.

The wolf darted off. They could still catch the raptors if they hurried, and now that the human was on a horse, they could travel much faster.

The wolf and the horse ran alongside each other. (He found a sweet spot, about thirty feet away, that didn't upset the Paint Horse.)

What joy the wolf felt in his heart, to participate in the chase with another hunter at his side! He'd waited all his life for this feeling. He ran through the snow, sucking in the cold wind and relishing the moment. The pack hunt was everything he'd ever hoped for and more.

If they ran quickly, they could use that speed to sequester one of the raptors from the other two. The two hunters crossed the undulating mountaintops. In the distance, the three Utahraptors appeared.

The wolf wondered how to tell the human which direction to go. If they were wolves, they would split left and right, and the movement of their bodies alone would guide the pack.

The human pointed to his right. It reminded the giant wolf of the Allosauruses, and how sometimes they would point with their heads before they attacked a herd of plant-eaters.

Finally! The human was using words.

The wolf split left while the horse and the human veered right. The wolf charged up the middle of the raptors. They were all sprinting now, and as he thought, raptors were not as fast as wolves, and they didn't have wolf stamina.

Jonah sneered at Warg. The wolf ignored the leader of the pack. He wanted the one with the sagging gut. He snapped his jaws at the raptor's legs. They were nothing more than a blur to him at these speeds. The raptor barked angrily and tried to slash him with her sickle, but the wolf was behind her. He couldn't be slashed. The raptor moved away from the other two.

The wolf was so happy. He pushed her back toward the human, who was barreling toward the raptor now. The hunter raised his bow and arrow. He'd never fired from the top of a galloping horse. His shot was clumsy and flew too high.

The wolf slammed into the raptor. He grabbed hold of flesh and shook it in his mouth with all his might.

The raptor screamed her pain. She sounded like a pig being electrocuted. She cut at the wolf's meaty belly. The wolf refused to let go. He was going to get this one. Whatever else happened that day, he couldn't say, but this raptor was going to die.

As is often the case with life, the victor becomes the victim. The other two raptors slammed into the wolf's sides. The wolf retaliated with a swift kick, but now it was his turn to run.

He caught up to the horse, which was having trouble in this section of the rocky mountainside. The raptors ran to their left and to their right. They maintained their distance until the wolf and the rider entered more forest. Now it was the raptors' territory. Using the trees to protect them, the raptors lunged at the animals, snapping and biting from the gaps between the trees. The horse, which had never settled, screamed and went into full panic mode. It kicked at the nearest raptor. The raptor easily dodged the horse's hoof.

The horse ran faster with very little control from its rider. The wolf was concerned, too. Had his pack bitten off more than they could chew? What had gone wrong? They were supposed to be chasing the raptors, not the other way around!

CHAPTER SEVEN

Cowboys and dinosaurs, this was not. I white-knuckled the horse's reins. The horse snorted as it flicked its ears and kicked. I felt less like a horseman and more like an amateur bronco rider trying to survive his first rodeo. I wished I had more experience riding horses, but I hadn't ridden since my childhood. I pulled back on the reins, but the horse shook its head aggressively. He was going to fight me.

All I could do was hold on. The horse did everything else. With its next kick, which again missed a raptor, I was bucked off. I landed into the snow and reached for an arrow.

Thankfully, the raptors didn't stop for me. Only Warg looked back, confusion spreading across his face, but he didn't wait. The wild hunt continued.

I checked my arms and legs. No broken bones, not even a busted rib. By some miracle, my bow and most of my arrows survived the fall, too.

From my prone position in the snowbank, the figures ahead appeared as two large black dots and three smaller red dots. All the dots ran toward the cliff. Then very quickly, the dots grew bigger until they were no longer dots anymore.

Warning alarms blared in my foggy head. *Get out of the way, stupid!*

The horse rushed right over me. I rolled in the nick of time as the hooves thundered past. A raptor lashed out, but I avoided its claws, too.

The horse and the wolf changed direction, once more sweeping toward me. This time, I stood my ground. I steadied an arrow, primed for the kill. I had to be patient. The raptors needed to be closer. They were all making a giant circle back to me. The horse was too scared to leave the mountaintop, so they were all swinging back and forth like a pendulum in hell.

Fine. I could do this. I had to wait until the raptors were in range. Some archers might fire a few shots ahead of the dinosaurs to "hone in" their shot. But since these arrows were my only weapon to protect me, I didn't want to waste a shot.

I wind-checked my ears and nose and felt a light wind blowing at me. I verified my assessment with the trees. No cross wind that I could determine. Using my sighting pins, I tracked the shot. I waited a bit longer to accommodate for the wind I'd be shooting into.

I fired. The arrow soared. Remember when I said I was a decent shot, but no expert Robin Hood/Hawkeye type? The arrow struck a stump in the middle of the action. I missed!

Again!

Half a second later, the circus of calamity raced around me. Every second counted. This could not go on much longer. Soon, my luck would run out and a raptor's talon or a horse's hoof would strike me a death blow.

I scanned the forest for anything that could help us escape.

"Warg!" I yelled. "WARG!" The wolf caught his name and veered toward me. The horse followed, not because it liked the wolf but because it was scared to death of the raptors.

Since I was farther away, I had a few seconds of buffer before they were right on top of me again. I led them into the trees to a fallen log. As I suspected, the wolf leaped over it, but the panicky horse slammed through. Old pine exploded, hitting the raptors and knocking them over. The horse stumbled. As the horse slowed, I grabbed onto the saddle horn and jumped on, clinging to the pommel. To fall would mean being killed by the raptors.

Luck was on my side cause hallelujah, it worked. The raptors were too tired. They needed to find one of their stashes and feed before they came after us again. I slowed the horse down. It was breathing heavy. I soothed it, repeating "Good boy. Take it easy," while rubbing the horse's sides.

The wolf was not impressed.

"Next time, we need a better plan," I said to Warg, who cocked his head questioningly.

CHAPTER EIGHT

The cold sun fought against its evening death, but it no longer possessed the stamina to remain upright in the sky. It collapsed into the mountains, whose jagged peaks stabbed at it like assassins lying in wait. The sun's body bled out, soaking the mountains in crimson light as it paled and then died. Purple shadows seized what was left of the sun's remains and dragged them down behind the mountains where they could be devoured in leisure.

"At least that's how I'd put it," I told Warg. I put the last log onto the small fire I erected for us. Warg ignored me but watched the horse, which was tied to a tree. The Paint nibbled at dry grass that pushed through the snow.

As Warg watched the horse, he licked his lips.

"Hey," I said emphatically. "He's not dinner."

Warg didn't look convinced, so I reiterated, "That's Bill the Pony. I know he's bigger than a pony, but he's my ride, so I can name him what I want, and you can't eat him."

I scrambled through my pack for the last of my venison and tossed it to Warg. He nudged the sticks, then slurped them up. He then rolled back onto his side to sleep.

Warg's chest rose and lowered with his breaths. I'd been living with this wolf for more than two days now, and I still hadn't gotten over how big he was.

"Bill, how do you think Warg got so big?"

Bill the Pony didn't say much as he munched the dead grass.

"I mean, look at him. It's so bizarre. I've been thinking about it all day. Except of course, for when I wasn't chasing or being chased by raptors. I have a theory based on what that woman was saying. Do you want to hear it?"

Bill flicked his tail.

"She called it *punctuated evolution*. I remember reading about wolves like him, Mackenzie River Wolfs. They're the largest wolves in the world, and they live in Canada. They were introduced to Yellowstone, but now they live in most national parks in the west, including what once was Dinosaur Falls National Park. People think they got so big because the prey was so big, meaning elk and bison. Take that same wolf and place it with dinosaurs, the largest animals to ever roam the planet, and the wolf suddenly grows bigger."

Bill snorted.

"Don't be like that. It makes sense. What will really Boggle your head are those cuts in his sides. I saw the blades on the ends of the raptors' claws, and I've witnessed up close what they can do to flesh. Those raptors should've carved through him like a Christmas turkey, but they didn't. His skin is stronger than any other mammal. Is that because of the dinosaurs, too?"

As I wondered aloud, I crept closer to Warg. I came up beside him. I reached out to touch his hide. Warg's golden eyes suddenly opened.

You bet I hesitated. "You gonna let me touch you, good boy?"

Warg didn't say anything. He watched me with that expressionless face of his.

My hand passed through Warg's hairs. Again I thought of a vast gray wheat field. "Good boy," I said.

"Grrrrr…"

"Okay, boy. Guess we're not there yet. I get it." I withdrew my hand. Warg stared at me a little longer, daring me to touch him, then his head flopped back down with a sigh of exhaustion.

I checked the saddle I'd removed from Bill earlier. I hoped to find something about the rider.

The leatherwork was intricately detailed. A hooded skull, a *Santa Muerte*, was cut into the pommel. The leather sheath strapped to the saddle was missing its unlimbered rifle. The two saddlebags, however, contained food and supplies I could use. Dried *papas*, *tortillas*, and more venison. I was growing tired of venison, but the *tortillas* and *papas* were sweet nourishment, even cold. The other bag was full of food for the horse. Each plastic bag was labelled with a different day of the week. This woman had intended to be out in the mountains for four or five days.

Since my gear was shambles, I added what was still usable to the saddle bag, then tossed my pack. It wasn't much anymore than a few pockets hanging from an internal frame. Maybe I should've been more sentimental about the pack. It'd traveled with me to every continent not named Antarctica, had logged hundreds of days on expeditions, and once was home to a lemur. But the most important memories would be all the overnights I did with Izzy and Kianne. Yosemite, Joshua Tree, perhaps twenty or thirty trips to Henry Cowell Redwoods State Park. A few multi-days on the Pacific Coast Trail and John Muir Trail. Kianne slipped and twisted her ankle on the Pacific Coast Trail. It not healing is what eventually led to her cancer diagnosis.

Still, equipment is just that: it's equipment. And when it's broken or no longer functional, it should be discarded. That's why you have to take care of it, like my bow and arrows. If anything, I felt guilty for leaving trash in the restricted area. I was always raised to pack-it-in, pack-it-out. But these were extraordinary times, and I had other work to perform.

I took the horse brush out and attended to Bill. I needed to make sure all the sweat was off Bill. The sweat would freeze, and a hypothermic horse was no good to me.

"At least you're getting used to ole Warg. Your owner must have kept dogs."

It was dark now, and from behind me came a low, short howl. While I'd been checking the saddle bags, the Wolf Moon had risen high over the trees. The moon was like a giant explosion in the sky blackening all the forest trees and casting shadows that shouldn't have existed after nightfall. It gave the mountain a luminescent, other-world quality.

"You're not a dog," I said to Warg. "But you're not a wolf, either."

Warg howled again. His voice was powerful, but his call was lonesome.

"You're just a lost soul looking for a place to belong." I cupped my hands over my mouth and howled my loudest.

Warg stopped and watched me howl. To be honest, Warg's gaze made me nervous. I wondered if I'd just crossed a line. Clearly, touching was off the board, but was howling, too? Had I offended him? Then again, hadn't I heard stories of people howling with coyotes and the coyotes responding?

So I tried again, doing my best to imitate Warg. Warg walked over to me. I stopped and stared at him and he stared back at me. Before I could say anything, he nuzzled me, tail wagging.

"Good Warg," I said, howling again. Warg joined me with a loud, booming howl.

People lived all their lives hoping for the kind of animal contact I was receiving. The exuberance overwhelmed me. I put my arms around

Warg's solid shoulders and brushed the soft fur. The skin underneath was as rough as packed concrete.

Warg growled sharply. I jumped back. "Okay. Still not touching. Got it." I howled again. Warg hesitantly joined me. Moonlight bathed over us.

In the distance, a sharp electric cry shot up from the forest. The blasphemous, electric howl was a mockery to everything we stood for.

Bill neighed his discomfort.

When the other raptors joined the first, I took a moment and steeled myself (that unnatural noise was always frightening) before I said, "They're getting farther away." Seeing Warg's concern, I added, "They won't escape."

CHAPTER NINE

The next morning, I ate the woman's venison jerky and brushed some of the peppercorn out of my new beard growth. Warg and I hit the trail before sunrise. The trees above us reminded me of knives pointing to the sky. The wolf led me deeper into the mountains.

"The farther I get from that parking lot, Bill, the more I doubt our odds of surviving."

New Profanity Peak jutted out of the surrounding mountainscape like a bad tooth that needed to be pulled. That mountain was the reason I didn't like our chances of survival. I hadn't realized how close we were to the Wildlife Restricted Area. I've read the reports of all the people who've died there. Time Magazine famously labeled Dinosaur Falls "the most dangerous place in the world," and that was the same year the US invaded Venezuela.

I didn't want to enter Dinosaur Falls, but the closer we got to New Profanity, the more I had to prepare myself for the likelihood. We were hunting dinosaurs after all.

My question was, why were we going back to Dinosaur Falls? The raptors had roamed outside the restricted area for months. Where they hunted was their territory. So why return? Was there something special in Dinosaur Falls? Or were they just leading us to familiar territory where they could confront us?

Bill snorted his disapproval.

"Oh, if you think that's bad, let me tell you a new theory I had this morning when I woke up. It's about how most animals went extinct at the end of the ice age. Pay attention, Bill. Back when proto-humans and Neanderthals ran around the world, we killed off all the giant animals, the mammoths, the giant sloths, the saber-toothed cats. I used to think like everyone else that we killed them for the meat. Now, I've changed my mind. I think it's 'cause we feared them. We couldn't stand living in a world where those monsters existed. That's not new. I've been developing that theory for a couple of days now. But the twist is this: now we've brought them back, only worse 'cause they're dinosaurs instead of mammoths. Dinosaurs don't give a type shit-o-negative about our problems, Bill. Your owner was killed, my daughter was shot, but the dinosaurs don't care. They don't even care about the food in the hunt. That makes them murderers, not hunters."

By mid-day Warg had tracked the raptors to a broken section of the fence surrounding the restricted area.

Entering the restricted area, I was breaking numerous federal laws. But this hunt had turned Survival Mode on...where I counted my victories in steps and breaths...and then to be partnered with this strange creature.... You have to understand, I felt as far from society as any person could. The chain link fence did not mark the gateway to federal property because federal property is a known entity. It is inventoried and regulated and overseen. This metal mesh showed the border between the wilderness as it should be and a darker, poisoned landscape: a hidden land of monsters whose existence was a betrayal to the universe.

The United States did not exist here. California might as well have been on a different continent. Ignore the sign hanging by a wire to the chain link and ignore the name it gives this place. This was New Profanity.

In this world, I'd been remade and given a new purpose. Social regulations and dogma no longer applied to me. I didn't think about the kids the raptors had killed, not like the Sheriff. And I wasn't seeking revenge for Jan and Mad Dog. What pulled me across this threshold would be the behavior of the raptors. Their senseless killing. Their need to destroy simply for the sake of destruction.

Hunting these beasts was for Izzy because her dying was as pointless as life could get.

Warg trotted inside the confines of the restricted area. He led us up the scarred side of New Profanity. The black rocks there looked like scabs, and the snow was pus-yellow and brown. The whole mountain appeared as if it was covered in contagion.

And despite all this, I was more concerned about the "protected" animals.

"Why are dinosaurs protected, Warg? Seems silly to think that dinosaurs need anybody's protection." My words sounded like something Mad Dog would say.

I watched the skies and listened to the forest. Every branch snapping was a Tyrannosaurus Rex, and any distant shape in the sky a pterosaur. This place and these monsters were getting under my skin and making me wary. I say that as someone who's hunted man-killing lions in Lindi.

We ascended New Profanity through clouds that rolled in, covering the landscape up here in misty haze. I could no longer see the valleys below or the picturesque Perdidos Mountains in the distance. A thin layer of haze hovered three feet off the ground, cutting the wolf and Bill and me in half.

The giant wolf stopped at a pile of rocks to sniff the ground. I scanned the area ahead, but didn't see anything except a large den. "Are they in there, Warg?"

That was impossible. The black hole in the rocks was too small to hold three person-sized raptors.

My answer lay not far from the den: the disarticulated skeleton of the largest wolf I'd ever seen aside from Warg. Warg wouldn't move closer to the den until I dismounted Bill and walked over.

Warg whined as he sniffed the skull.

Closer to the den lay several smaller skeletons. Puppies. My heart was breaking.

"That's your Mom, isn't it?" I asked. I picked up a blanched rib. A large gash cut through the bone. "The raptors attacked your den. The world squishes mothers and fathers, and now you want your vengeance."

Warg's golden eyes shined more golden than ever, like they burned with angel fire. I understood that flame. "I thought animals weren't supposed to be vengeful, but you're not a regular animal, are you? Vengeance is a language you and I share. I'm going to help you give these raptors what they deserve. Between your claws and my arrows, we'll kill them all. But why would the raptors come back here? I doubt there was any surplus kill here. So why return? Psychological terror?"

My mouth dropped open. "Those sons of bitches, Warg. They chased me for a day just to chase me. They wouldn't kill me. They gutted Mad Dog and left him to die in front of me. Those sons of bitches. They're doing all of this just to mess with our heads. They want us scared and despondent. They are literally dragging up our worst memories. These things have to die." I was starting to see the point of what the woman had told me. There were no creatures on Earth like raptors, and maybe they were more like a plague than an animal.

That's when the electricity howled. The raptors were mimicking their howls from last night. Taunting us from the trees.

I notched an arrow against my bowstring and aimed into the trees. I remembered this tactic. Fool me once, shame on you. Fool me twice…

"Bring it, you tree climbing cowards!"

A tree crashed somewhere up ahead. The thud of the tree's fall shook the ground. I nearly lost my arrow.

They weren't taunting Warg. Not taunting at all. This was new. What were they up to?

Another tall pine crashed and fell. This one was much closer, on the other side of the den. The tree broke into pieces as it smashed against the mountain rocks.

A giant rectangular head full of sharp teeth pushed through the foliage behind the den. The T. Rex smiled dangerously.

I'd never encountered an animal so large and so damn powerful. Its leg muscles were longer than a bear. Keep that at the bottom of your temporal lobe. This was the dinosaur everybody thought of when they said "dinosaur." And it was big enough to shove trees aside with its clawed feet.

I've heard people talk about the "T. Rex's majesty." That's bullshit. There was nothing majestic or royal about this king carnivore. T. Rexes are more like teeth puking teeth adorned with talons, but in a sacrilegious way.

Being disemboweled by this monster while it ate me would be anything but dignified. Gangbanged by knives was probably more accurate.

And if you're one of those people who glorify T. Rex kills into some nature-channel beautiful thing....First, go to hell. There's nothing admirable about one animal killing another. It's food, plain and simple. Second, the T. Rex's predatory gaze on me was less like a lion hunting gazelles and more like a serial killer or pedophile stalking their next victim.

This was the singular most devastating creature I'd ever seen in my entire life. And I might as well have been standing naked in front of it.

Five more heads appeared next to the first one. Ten sets of evil eyes scowled down at me, Bill, and Warg. If I'd done a better job at staying hydrated, I would've pissed my pants.

My voice gave out as I squeaked, "Run, Warg!"

CHAPTER TEN

Warg was already gone, running so fast he seemed to glide down the mountainside. The way he was sprinting before any of us, he must've had run-ins with T. rexes in his life. Bill galloped at the giant wolf's side. Rider-less, I will add.

"Come back!" I yelled. But Bill had as much intention of helping me as he did of sharing glue recipes with the T. Rexes. Down to one play left, I aimed for an eye and fired. The arrow landed with a *thunk* in the dinosaur's thick head. The T. Rex roared angrily.

Good, I thought. *Come a little closer.* I re-aimed for the eye. The arrow weaved through the air and made a wet, splashy sound. The T. Rex shook his giant head, moaning. Imagine the sound of a jet engine turning on, then exploding. That's the closest comparison I can make to the sound that came out of the T. Rex's mouth. The monster fell back, but four additional T. Rexes appeared. It was an entire herd. *An entire god-damned herd!*

I bolted down the side of the mountain. The rocky terrain hindered my flight. Behind me, giant clawed feet slammed into the ground. I kept expecting them to bite me in half, but I dared not glance behind me. I could do the math. I took probably twenty steps for every one or two of theirs. There was only one way to escape them, and that was over the side of the mountain.

So this is where I die.

I closed my eyes as I ran toward the peak's edge. From the accounts of a pair of mountain climbers who scaled New Profanity's eastern face, I knew there was a thousand-foot drop.

Suddenly, a mouth lifted me up off my feet. I cringed and waited for the death-dealing bite, but the final crunch never came. Instead, I bounced around in the air. The T. Rexes roared behind me. Finally, I opened my eyes.

Warg held me up off the ground, carrying me like a puppy by the back of my shirt. Together we careened down the side of the mountain.

As terrified as I was, a part of me awed at my predicament. Had anyone ever felt the bond between human and animal so strongly? Warg came back for me. He had to race into mortal peril to help me. And if he had not done that, I'd have been Tyrannosaurus snacks.

That didn't mean I was safe. An avalanche of T. Rexes slammed down the side of the mountain behind us. I counted thirty or more heads now, all incensed. "Faster, Warg! Faster!"

RRRRIIIIIIIP!

All that stress on my jacket, and the collar separated from the shoulder lining. I fell butt-first into the snow. Warg fell on top of me. We had come far, almost all the way down the side of the mountain.

If I'd had time, I would have stopped and taken in the beauty of the dinosaur herds grazing languidly through the valley. I was actually there, in Dinosaur Falls. Some hunters considered this the Happy Hunting Grounds. Around beers, we'd tell stories of all the dinosaurs we would hunt, and we would laugh about trying to create trophies of their heads. How do you mount a Triceratops head?

Bill was struggling in the trees not far from me. I dashed to Bill's side.

The tyrannosaurs rumbled downward. They roared violence. They were maybe 30 meters away.

Out of the corner of my eye, I glimpsed the raptors on the far sides of the herd. Those sadistic monsters were steering the T. Rexes toward us!

I didn't have time to be angry. I needed to free Bill and then climb into the saddle. I'd been lucky with Warg. I wouldn't be that lucky twice.

Because nature had a sense of humor for that horse, Bill's reins were caught on a tree branch.

"Thank God for your bad luck," I said, unwrapping the reins. I jumped onto Bill before the Paint Horse could run off. I swept my leg over Bill's side and shoved a hiking boot into a stirrup.

"Let's go!"

Bill swept into the valley, the giant carnivores chasing close behind.

A T. Rex snapped its jaws around me, barely missing because I rolled to Bill's side. It was a move I'd never repeat again in my lifetime, and I'm still not quite sure how I managed it. I've seen movie cowboys pull that stunt, but I have no idea how I did it. I guess the adrenaline rush of survival makes us better than we are.

Another T. Rex clamped down on Bill's tail but caught only horse hairs. A few hoof beats later, the horse and wolf separated from the T. Rexes. They were too fast for the herd to keep up.

But there was a new problem. In their flight, they'd caught up to the herds in the valley, who had seen the herd of T. Rexes and now were also fleeing from the rolling carnage.

I couldn't see through the clouds of snow kicked up from the stampede. I waved the snow out of my face. A massive tail, perhaps from the Apatosaurus, swooped over me. It was like dodging a redwood tree trunk. I remembered how Bill handled tree trunks by plowing straight through them. I hoped we wouldn't have to jump any tails. I ducked in time to avoid the Apatosaurus.

Gargantuan shadows appeared in the snow cloud. They didn't make me feel any better about our predicament.

Bill seemed able to avoid being struck. Warg adopted some form of dino-parkour, jumping off the backs of slow-moving Ankylosauruses and weaving between the legs of taller dinosaurs. That wolf never ceased to amaze me. I was beginning to understand how much the park influenced him, growing up here. I wondered what it was like living among the dinosaurs. I imagined it was brutal.

I didn't have time to admire the giant wolf in his element. I pulled hard left before Bill impaled himself while barging through a Stegosaurus tail. As Bill moved left, a T. Rex head appeared. Sharp teeth bit down onto the Stegosaurus tail. The Stegosaurus shook its injured tail, splattering blood all over me and the nearby dinosaurs. The Stegosaurus slowed down behind me. I glanced back. Another T. Rex pounced on it. The Stegosaurus uttered a vicious hiss that sounded like crackling television static.

The Stegosaurus turned sideways to the oncoming horde. It tried to swing its horns, but the T. Rex refused to let go. A second T. Rex appeared and bit the Stegosaurus on the side. I couldn't watch.

I turned around in time to not be impaled by a phalanx of Triceratops. Dozens of horns emerged out of the blurred snow, horns facing into the horde. One mother charged me and Warg, her head low to the ground.

Warg jumped right. Bill, who seemed highly skilled in self-preservation, had enough sense to not blast through the dinosaur that was at least three times his size. Bill dodged left and we circled around the group. Just in time, we escaped into the protection of the phalanx with the other herbivores. The Triceratops were backing into trees, where it would be difficult for the T. Rexes to attack. Seconds after we entered, the phalanx closed. Directly behind the ring of Triceratops stood all kinds of long-necked dinosaurs: Apatosauruses, a pod of Diplodocuses, and a few shorter-necked duckbilled dinosaurs. There was even a group of Ankylosauruses, though I had no idea what good they would do anyone behind the Triceratops.

Bill found a spot between the duckbills, which were mostly Parasaurolophus and Edmontosaurus dinosaurs. They had crests or large rounded horns curling from the backs of their heads. I didn't argue with Bill. We both caught our breath. We were safe for the moment. The plant-eaters weren't kicking us out. Warg snuck in next to me, panting as well. For the first time, his side was completely pressed against my leg. I patted him on the shoulders, and he didn't growl or snap at me.

The duckbilled dinosaurs grumbled their disapproval of the giant wolf, but as long as Warg didn't make any sudden moves, the duckbills didn't freak out.

Bill's breathing was getting deeper and deeper. He had to work to breath. I needed to get off him so that he could calm down, but then I'd be too low to see the incoming T. Rexes.

"I'm sorry, Bill. I'll get off as soon as I can. Just a bit longer."

The army of herbivores bleated threats that sounded like an Air Force of electric planes.

The falling snow did not answer back, and for a moment I thought we'd escaped the T. Rexes, but then the unmistakable shadows of two-legged dinosaurs appeared in the snow. As the kicked-up snow finished falling back to the ground, the Tyrannosaurus warriors appeared with barbarian ferocity. Some were covered in the blood of their victories; others in the wounds of their defeat. Battle-hungry and starved for meat in the middle of the dark winter, the T. Rexes surveyed the phalanx, searching for an opening.

Next to the thirty Tyrannosauruses, the valley's bachelor herd of Allosauruses joined. They snapped their elongated jaws at the herd. My heart sank. Battles like these were not as rare as people wanted to believe. Giant herds had been facing off like this since before humans existed.

"This is my first dinosaur battle royale, Warg. Any suggestions?"

Rip their hearts out and don't die, Warg's face said. It was every *you're the wolf, not the sheep* inspirational poster you've ever seen. No lie, his angry face comforted me. I'm a hunter, not a warrior, but I'd taken many lives before. With Warg at my side, I could survive this.

"Well, if this is how I'm going out, I guess a dinosaur battle is as good as any."

Several T. Rexes charged from different angles. The Triceratops held their ground, swaying their horns and frills dangerously, like sabers at the giant meat eaters. The T. Rexes backed off before they got close.

One didn't stop soon enough. He got too close. He was punished not by the Triceratops's rattling saber, but by a giant whip tail that cracked at his head. The sound was like a clap of thunder. The T. Rex stumbled. The Triceratops charged him, spearing the T. Rex with his horns. Gore bubbled down the spikes beneath its frill. Several long dinosaur necks shot out from behind the phalanx and bit at the T. Rex's head. The T. Rex shook his head, then stumbled back to the horde. He fell, a lifeless form on the battlefield.

My jaw dropped. I couldn't believe they'd just taken out a Tyrannosaurus Rex. You always think of the "Tyrant King" as the apex predator of the dinosaur world, and I'm not saying they aren't, but just because a T. Rex was powerful didn't mean the other dinosaurs weren't armed and dangerous. I had a newfound respect for this herd. I also wondered if I was safer here than on the other side. As long as they didn't perceive me as a threat, I guessed I was safest being among them.

That loss of life might have been enough to deter predators during a spring or summer attack, but this was the middle of winter, and food was scarce. The giant carnivores were low on options, and the odds were against them. Like most meat eaters, their attacks were successful less than ten percent of the time.

Me, I was pumped 'cause of what I just witnessed. I believed we had a chance to escape. I drew an arrow and scanned the crowd of carnivores. They were too far away to hit, but I wanted to be ready. The next T. Rex that got too close was going to get an arrow in the heart.

Scanning the crowd of carnivores, I realized then that I didn't see any of the raptors. Where had they gone?

The trees! I turned Bill around, which was not easy to do in the best of situations, but in a crowd of large dinos, it was even harder. Bill turned reluctantly. The horse didn't understand why anyone wouldn't want to keep an eye on the horde. But being in a herd of herbivores helped settle him, even if they weren't of the same species.

I spotted a clawed hand up in the trees. It was barely visible on the bark. To everyone else in the herd, it was perfectly camouflaged, but a lifetime of hunting taught me what to look for. I unleashed the arrow. The broadpoint found the raptor's malicious hand and nailed it to the tree. The raptor pulled back, but was stuck to the tree. It screamed electric fury.

"Got him!"

Jonah and the bulging raptor jumped down behind the herd. Jonah landed on a duckbill next to me. The bulging raptor landed on an Apatosaurus. Their sickle cuts were vicious, but they were too few in numbers to do anything but get themselves killed. They didn't intend to slay. The point was to startle the army into breaking rank.

It worked.

Chaos thundered and trampled in a stampede of fear. The Apatosaurus charged forward in pain, shoving a Triceratops aside. The Triceratops bellowed in shock, then ran in another direction. Dinosaurs broke rank. The horde of T. Rexes saw their chance and attacked.

I was intent on killing that raptor in the tree, though.

It's about confidence, I told Izzy when she missed hitting the stag. *You have to believe you can hit the target before you shoot. If you don't believe in your shot, you will miss.*

Alright, Daddy.

I pulled back on the bowstring. Felt its weight settling into my back muscles. Rooting into my spine. It was the same weight of pain I carried for my daughter's death. I didn't need the pins. I couldn't see the raptor because it was hidden in the trees. But I believed in my shot, and I tapped into something unexplainable.

I released the arrow.

The pointed shaft weaved through the air the way that good arrows will, like they are cutting the air. A long Diplodocus head lifted out of the din and chaos, nearly knocking my arrow off its course. Diplodocus head and arrow did not connect, though. The arrow sailed over. Disappeared into the pines.

The raptor dropped from the tree, my arrow buried in its chest.

Time had slowed for the shot. The raptor seemed to plummet for ages. Once its body disappeared behind the other dinosaurs, though, time shot forward.

Dinosaurs rumbled all around me.

It was all Warg and I could do to not get squashed between the mountains of meat. In the fray of battle, I lost track of the other two raptors, Jonah and the plump-bellied one.

Suddenly, Bill jumped aside. I was about to chastise him, but then the Draconyx rushed right through the space we'd just occupied. In jumping, Bill bounced off the back leg of a Triceratops. The Paint Horse decided he'd had enough. He reared up and ran us out into the open fields.

God bless us, this horse and his sense of self-preservation was going to kill me yet!

CHAPTER ELEVEN

As soon as Bill broke the line, the meat eaters lunged for him. They may have never seen a horse before, but T. Rexes weren't finicky eaters. Anything that ran from them was lunch, and Bill served them up the chase. Two giant Tyrannosaurus Rexes pursued us.

On his best days, the horse was the fastest creature in North America's animal kingdom. Nothing could outrun or outlast it, not even wolves. This was not Bill's best day. He was scared, and he'd been surviving on adrenaline for a long time. Horses, being flight animals, produce more than ten times the levels of adrenaline as other animals, and they don't know when to stop. The lactic acid was built up in Bill's legs, and his lungs were on fire. His heart pounded so heavily, it seemed about to rip him apart.

I had no choice but to jump off him and make a run for the line. If I was lucky, the T. Rexes wouldn't chase me.

For once, I was lucky. I made it back as an Allosaurus slashed at me with his open mouth. It expanded so wide, it seemed unhinged. His gaping jaws reminded me of a striking cottonmouth I'd encountered in the Everglades. Four-inch-long daggers should have stabbed me, but Warg pulled the Allosaurus by the tail. It was just enough to allow me to retreat back to safety.

The Allosaurus turned on Warg, but the wolf was fast, and he'd been dealing with Allosauruses all his life. He climbed up the theropod and jumped, landing beside me.

Dino-parkour!

Bill charged into the trees. The two T. Rexes closed in on him.

I couldn't watch. Besides, I had bigger problems. The army of herbivores was spreading too thin. The Triceratops moved to one side, making the giant long-necked dinosaurs vulnerable to leaping

Allosauruses. The Diplodocuses and Apatosauruses pushed the Ankylosauruses forward, forcing them outside the phalanx.

No matter how armored an Ankylosaurus was, I didn't believe they had a chance against the horde. Meat eaters quickly surrounded them.

But then the Ankylosauruses did something unexpected. As the T. Rexes surrounded them, the smaller dinosaurs stamped in the snow and mud. Half of them turned about-face until they were binarily positioned. Two Ankylosauruses faced one direction, and the other two faced in the opposite direction. They swung their gigantic clubbed tails side to side. Since the front end of the Ankylosaurus was lower than the back end, their heads were in no danger of being accidentally clubbed. The two on the sides leaned inward, creating a giant, domed shell protected by swinging clubs.

Will wonders never cease? I've seen some crazy things, but never this.

The T. Rexes were puzzled by the change in behavior. They began thrusting their massive heads at the dinosaur tank. They were trying to catch something fleshy, but here there was nothing tender or timid. Their fangs found fierce armor covered in spikes and nodes. After the first near hit, the kings of the dinosaur world gave up.

Better to find easier prey.

CHAPTER TWELVE

Something large and full of teeth made a desperate leap over the broken Triceratops line, completely destroying the herd's protection. Dinosaurs scattered, and it was only by luck that my butt escaped alive. I got the lead out, as my grandfather would say, and fled deep into the forest.

I didn't see which direction Warg went, which alarmed me. I hoped he was safe and that we would meet up later after we'd escaped.

Trees exploded around me as dinosaurs toppled over each other in their fights for survival. Behind me, an Apatosaurus lifted its heavy front legs at a T. Rex. I thought of deer rising up on their rear legs to ward off attackers with their hooves. Head first, the T. Rex bashed the Apatosaurus in its chest. The Apatosaurus fell backwards. Its long body rolled toward me. I ran faster.

I turned away from where I thought the head would land. I guessed wrong. That long neck came down on me like a falling skyscraper. I couldn't get away. The dinosaur's large head smashed the ground beside me with enough force to knock me off my feet.

When Izzy was little, we owned a trampoline. I was out with her, watching her. In her excitement she wasn't paying attention. She was four or five years old at this point. The trampoline gave her a bad bounce and she landed right beside me. The sound of her leg bone cracking is a sound that will haunt me for the rest of my days. I was so guilt-ridden. We rushed her to the hospital. We didn't get home until late that night. I put Izzy to bed, and then I disassembled the trampoline and tossed it in the garbage.

Hitting the ground, the Apatosaurus's head made the same sound Izzy's leg made that day on the trampoline. To say I felt the bone break in my soul sounds like hyperbole, but it wasn't much of a stretch. I winced. The Apatosaurus made a startled sound and then was silent. The

T. Rex jumped at the dinosaur's exposed belly. I needed to escape the carnage. I stumbled back upright and kept running. I ran for a long time.

At some point I realized the cries had stopped. Either the slaughter was over, or I'd run so far I couldn't hear them anymore. I bent over, took several deep breaths, then looked back over my shoulder into the trees.

Nothing. Just blowing wind.

Something didn't feel right. I checked to my left and to my right.

A giant T. Rex stood there watching me, its tiny hand on a branch twenty feet up in the air. Let me tell you, that hand did not seem so tiny in the wild! I stared at the T. Rex, wondering what it would do next.

It watched me. Again with the serial killer vibe.

Slowly, I reached behind for my compound bow. They didn't make a draw heavy enough for T. Rexes. Before my appearance here, bow hunting had never been tested on dinosaurs, so I had absolutely zero ounces of confidence that this arrow could puncture that T. Rex's heart. I'd seen my arrow barely puncture a T. Rex's skin.

I plucked one of the arrows from the quiver. It seemed hopeless, a meager arrow against a ten-ton eating machine. Have you watched those old dinosaur movies? People shooting ineffectively at dinosaurs with their rifles and pistols? Well, I had a pointed stick…

I didn't want to upset the T. Rex, so I didn't adjust my sighting pins. I pulled back on the bowstring, gave a hunter's guess, and aimed high.

For what felt like an hour, the world's largest land predator stared at me. People talk about the size of a T. Rex, but it's a whole other thing standing beneath one. Call them dragons, call them Godzilla. T. Rexes turn us into mice and voles.

I waited for the release.

After an intense minute or two of staring at each other, the T. Rex turned away and thundered back to the slaughter.

My legs went numb and I fell to the ground. I hoped I never saw another T. Rex again in my life.

Something furry pressed against the back of my head. Cold dread soured my stomach.

I turned around.

Warg watched me, his eyes communicating the need to hurry. The raptors were still out there.

Had we really come so far in such a short time that we could communicate with glances?

Warg nodded. I noticed the claw marks in the ground, too. Two sets of prints led away. We tracked the raptors through a large arch shrouded in snow to a different section of the park. Here, steam rose from geysers and boiling mud bubbled from pools. The hot air reeked of sulphur. Mineral leaching had blanched the bases of tree trunks a ghostly white.

I recognized this land. Original settlers had named the geysers Messina Springs, as innocuous a name as can be, but once Dinosaur Falls National Park was created, YouTube watchers redubbed this part of the park "The Hellpits." This name was a portmanteau of its nickname, the Hellscape Tarpits.

Full disclosure, there are no tarpits in Dinosaur Falls. That's just YouTubers being YouTubers.

Like bison in Yellowstone, dinosaurs gravitated to the Hellpits in winter, and people loved to watch the beauty of giant animals surrounded by snow and steam and the pretty-colored geysers. But like NASCAR, some viewers watched for the pleasure of the crash. Every once in a while, a large-bodied behemoth who was too heavy to be supported by the fragile landscape plopped to its death into a steaming geyser. The schadenfreude of the dinosaur's death always went viral. There were even entire YouTube channels devoted to dinosaur deaths in the Hellpits.

Warg and I weaved through the nightmarish landscape, careful to avoid the geysers. This was easier said than done. Geysers suddenly appeared out of the ground, and what once seemed easily treadable was suddenly dangerous. Warg's paw slipped, nearly sliding into a vat of acidic mud. The steam singed the hairs on his paws.

The Utahraptors emerged over a rise. Waves of heat bent and twisted their shapes into demonic forms. They didn't flee. Just stood in the open ground and watched us tracking them.

"What are they doing, Warg? Why aren't they hiding or attacking?"

Moments later, the answer appeared: a nest, but unlike any I'd ever seen. Instead of twigs and branches, this raptor nest was an amalgamation of bones and body parts. Elk antlers, deer ribs, and decayed human arms surrounded a clutch of four freshly laid eggs. The raptor with the bulge had been carrying eggs, not worms. Now that she laid them, she'd lost much of her girth. She'd also do anything to protect her new clutch.

They were using the routes between the restricted area and the outside world to build the kind of nest you imagined only happened in horror movies.

I began a hunter's prayer. "Lord, watch over me in this hellscape. Guide my arrows to the beasts of this unforgiving land."

A beautiful geyser of overlapping red and gold separated the raptors from us. Once again, Warg and I split up, each taking a different side of the geyser. We'd become such instinctual hunters together. A pack.

Looking at Warg, I said, "Grant me wisdom and respect in the hunt. Keep me humble in the harvest, and in the harvest, free me from worldly pursuits."

Step by careful step, we approached the raptors, who hadn't left the area. How could they? The survival of their blood lay on their success today. For them, this wasn't hunting or surplus killing. It was kill or be killed. Natural law. I remembered telling Mad Dog that raptors didn't obey the usual laws of nature. Sitting with Mad Dog and Jan in a tree seemed like a million years ago, when in reality only a few days had passed. I wasn't sure exactly how long ago. Time had become funny to me up here in the Perdidos. Time was as malleable as the truth.

Had I hunted raptors with a giant wolf? Was I in the middle of a restricted area infamous throughout the world for its kill count? Or was I simply a man who went crazy in the forest and lost my way like some ill-begotten Barclay's Marathon runner? I remembered Deputy Keener's warning that the lifespan of anyone entering the park was 44 hours. I hadn't technically entered the park until a few hours ago, yet the gravity of his warning weighed on me.

Walking toward the raptors was the third hardest walk of my life. It went against human nature to walk up to an animal that could easily tear me apart. Think about it. If you saw a tiger standing outside, would you walk up to it? When every cell in my heart and every fiber of my essence ordered me to run, I had to reject that command, push that fear far enough away from me so that I could keep moving forward to Jonah.

Every foot taken echoed the long walk I made past the wooden pews to the casket at my wife's burial. It was the hardest walk a man can make until he has to walk once more down the same aisle for his daughter's funeral. Atop one casket lay lilies, the other a Teddy Bear. In a way, their deaths had prepared me for this, but I'm not the kind of person to think that their senseless deaths happened so that I could kill the Utahraptors. To hell with the woman rider's comments about me being the last hope. If it'd been all for this, life was pain and there was no redemption for it. Period.

Perspiration dappled on my forehead and slid sticky as glue down the sides of my face. I felt it on my arms and the backs of my hands, too. The entire hunt had been moving to this single moment. Eons of wait followed by a spike of effort, skill, and adrenaline.

I didn't need a scope to tell me I was close enough to kill Jonah. I was working on instinct now.

I unleashed my arrow. It sailed ten yards, as straight and true as any arrow ever flew. Jonah leaped at me. The arrow hit Jonah sideways and glanced off his thick skin.

I shouted angrily against life for everything I missed: Jonah's kill, my wife, my daughter.

Without sympathy, Jonah crashed on top of me. This wasn't over yet. I didn't have time to beat my chest and scream long, drawn-out cries against life and all its failures. We fell over.

Jonah's burned face pressed close to mine, so close that I could feel the warmth emanating from his scar tissue. I'd heard this about burn victims, but never known it to be true until Jonah's mouth spread wide over my head.

I reached for the gut hook knife, but the leather tab on my fingers was in the way. Jonah raised his leg. The deadly curved scimitar protruded from the end of his toe. His protrusion reminded me of documentaries where I'd seen blowflies erupting from live tissue. There was something so sinister as the unsheathing of his claw.

I twisted my hand, got the knife, and slashed upward, cutting against the Utahraptor's toe as it pressed into my stomach.

Jonah vaulted away, screeching in pain. As Jonah kicked off, I stumbled backward and tripped on a rock. Rising steam warned me of what was to come, but I was off-balance and had no control. Have you ever turned and tripped on the edge of a step that you didn't see? One foot stays where it is, the other slams down hard. My boot sloshed in the hot mud rimming the geyser. Warmth embraced my foot. I couldn't save myself. Hands went straight down into the mud, but my face fell left-side-first into boiling water.

Out of my mouth came a sound like a rabbit being slaughtered, like a red fox screaming as it's torn apart by hounds. I'm not sure which it was more like, but all I know is, I couldn't make that sound again, not in a hundred years.

I jerked my face out of the geyser. Red and gold water sloshed off my face. I shoved it in the cool snow. I could literally feel my face bubbling with blisters. Even in the snow, it still burned.

When I looked up, I saw Warg. He stood still as he prepared to pounce on the mother raptor. His snout was lined up straight across from me. His face was every big, bad wolf ever described in words. I was glad I was on his side.

Too much anger at Jonah raged in me to feel anything but a numbness on the left side of my face. I dove at Jonah, the gut hook knife held over my head. I brought the blade down on that raptor. Jonah used my momentum and kicked me over. I tried to hook him with the knife. I somersaulted but came up on my feet. Again, I teetered on the edge of a geyser. This time I was able to avert a fall into the flaming hot water.

I checked Warg. Warg fought the mother, all fangs and claws.

When Warg backed off, two bright ribbons of blood appeared on his shoulders. Warg glanced over at me, wary of my attention.

Jonah raked a claw across my face and bit down on the arm holding the gut hook knife. *Stupid! Keep your eyes on your prey!*

"AAAAGH!" The raptor had the strength to bend iron traps. A few millimeters deeper, and his clawed hand would have cured me of an eye. I pounded my free arm on Jonah's head, then jammed my thumb in the raptor's eye. Jonah screamed and released me.

We backed up and away from each other to catch our breath. Reassess. As we circled, Jonah remained low, ready to attack at any moment. He made sure to keep his body between me and the eggs.

"I'm going to kill you, Jonah, and then I'm going to kill your brood, too. Give me that, and I'll stop. 'Cause you, you're every funeral I've ever attended. If you die, I'll never hunt again."

CHAPTER THIRTEEN

Warg looked over at the human who had become his packmate. The man was speaking again, this time to the raptor, but what was he saying? Once more the wolf wished the human could speak his language.

The mother took the opportunity to charge the wolf. She slashed at his legs, then ran to his side and darted away. She stopped after a few strides to make sure he followed her.

She was attempting to lure him away from the nest, and for now, the wolf was willing to go along with this. He could always come back for the nest later.

She ran out into the snow. He chased her. He was so close to avenging his family. If he could just catch her. And yet, the human was all he could think about. Something had changed in the hunter. It was like one moment he was still a puppy, and the next moment, he was an all-grown wolf. And like any wolf, he was ready to hunt for real. Warg thought maybe he, the wolf, was the prey. He was not a trusting animal by nature, but he wanted to trust this human. Their time together as a pack had meant more for the wolf than anything else in his life since his family was murdered.

The wolf glanced back over at the human. They were stealing looks at each other when they should be paying attention to the claws in front of them.

This human was always distracting him!

The mother kicked the wolf in the side. If he wasn't made of such strong skin, his bowels would be steaming in the snow below him. Warg was a lucky wolf. He couldn't make that mistake again.

He chased the mother around the geyser pits. As she ran, she kicked hot mud in his face. The mud burned. He shook his head. But the mud burned her feet, too. He could smell her rough skin cooking as much as his hairs.

She jumped over a wide, red and orange geyser pool. The wolf jumped it just as easily as she. The mother continued to lead him away, hoping to lose him in the geysers because she could leap so far. Unfortunately for her, the wolf could cross farther distances. She changed her tactic and began timing her jumps so that when he jumped, he'd be caught in a fountain of steaming, boiling water. Raptors are cunning.

So are wolves.

The wolf anticipated her leap and found a shorter distance to cross. He planned to get ahead of her. A vat of steam erupted, cooking his hide. He yelped in pain as he landed in the hot mud in front of her.

He'd cut her off, but not off-guard.

She attacked the wolf, her deadly talons flashing in the air. The wolf reached straight for her gut. He bit down on her stomach tissue and jerked it side to side. He ripped and ripped until her belly popped. She screamed defiantly. It sounded like he was being struck by lightning, but he kept on jerking from side to side until she wasn't fighting him anymore and he was just flinging her dead body around.

It felt so good to destroy her. A confession of pain.

Raptor dead, the wolf looked up. The human stood on a narrow bank between two pools. His bow and arrow were raised. Jonah had returned to the clutch of eggs, still wet from being laid. Jonah watched them both with deep concern. His head pivoted from the hunter on one side to the wolf on the other, and him in between.

The lips on the human frowned an immeasurable sorrow. He was sorry for the wolf, and for life, and for the daughter he'd lost. The human wore his daughter's death like a burdened coat.

The wolf knew more words than this human thought. He'd been listening. He wasn't just big. The woman was right. Something had happened to the animals in Dinosaur Falls, and maybe they were evolving to confront the dinosaurs, but now the wolf thought maybe they were evolving to fight humans, too.

The wolf ROARED his denial.

CHAPTER FOURTEEN

I couldn't believe what I heard. Did I hear it? *That's not real*, my mind said. That's your mental break. You're tilting at windmills, Don Quixote. Wolves don't understand language, and they certainly can't articulate feelings.

And yet, I couldn't escape the words of the woman rider. *Punctuated evolution*. Changing to meet the challenge of the dinosaurs.

The arrow flew. The fletching cut my cheek as the shaft launched from my bow. The arrow slid in a confident, serpentine rhythm though the air and bored into Jonah's leg. Jonah snarled. He snapped the arrow with his hand. He lowered his head and bared his teeth. The sound coming from the dinosaur's throat was the worst sound I'd ever heard.

I jumped up in excitement. My feet slid in the mud, but I quickly recovered. I did *not* want a replay of my faceplant.

I plucked another arrow from my quiver while Jonah charged.

I pulled back on the bowstring, drawing out the full weight of the mechanism. I'd stretched the string so deep, the barbed arrowhead grazed the edge of my fingers.

"Izzy, guide my arrow."

Steam from my breath lifted and joined the geyser vapors.

The arrow shot. Jonah leaped over the geyser.

CHAPTER FIFTEEN

As the giant wolf watched, the father raptor shot backward. The thrust of the second arrow impaled the monster's body to the ground. The wolf came around the side of the Utahraptor so that the beast could see him in the full. This thing killed his mother.

Jonah glanced from the eggs to the wolf. Snarling, he pushed himself up out of the arrow. A giant bubble of blood plopped onto the ground.

The two charged like jousters from a different age. They collided into each other and rolled around in the soft ground and snow. The wolf pinned Jonah to the ground. Jonah hiked his one good leg like a switchblade knife trying to slash the giant wolf's throat. The wolf dodged the talon and crushed the foot in his powerful jaws. The raptor screeched in pain. The wolf then snapped the bones in Jonah's other foot. He took his time, destroying every claw until the raptor could do nothing but writhe impotently. Then, his belly rumbling with the growls of a hundred hounds, the wolf dragged the raptor out into the snow and stood over him, posturing.

He sneered as he pressed harder against Jonah's windpipe. Jonah couldn't scream. The electric current of his wails flickered. Jonah's death was slow and difficult. Finally, the lights went out behind the raptor's eyes. A shadow fell over the dead raptor.

The wolf and the human stared at each other, both heaving frosted air. Then the lone wolf walked back to the nest and sniffed the four eggs. Looking the hunter in the eyes, the wolf kicked one into the geyser. The egg listed from side to side, then sunk into the boiling waters.

There were still three eggs, and the greatest vengeance was not the death of your enemies, but to raise their children and turn them against your enemies.

The wolf made several turns in the nest and lay down among the raptor eggs.

"No," the hunter said. "They have to die. I promised." Tears crisscrossed down his grimy face. They'd been through so much together. He didn't want it to end this way. "You killed one. Let's kill the others."

The wolf growled. The hunter plucked another arrow from his quiver while Warg stood up. He threatened the hunter with raised hackles and malevolent, golden eyes. They'd gone from strangers to hesitant partners to a wolf pack, and now the hunter was making them enemies. There was no coming back from this.

The string stretched. The arrow drew back. The energy tightened in his back and waited for release.

"Come on, Warg. Walk away. I don't want to shoot you."

Warg refused to move.

"The world squashes fathers and mothers."

Warg pushed one paw back defiantly. He'd made his choice.

"Don't do this."

Warg stepped forward and rested his chin on the tip of the arrow. Gently, he nudged the bowhunter's aim away from him and the eggs.

If he could see through the hunter's eyes, he wouldn't see a wolf pushing against the arrow, but a young girl's hand pulling it away.

"Izzy, I'm so sorry."

The hunter felt the power of the bowstring release through the anguish in his heart and the tears in his eyes.

"I can't stop it. I can't stop any of it."

There was right and there was wrong, and most times the wrong outlived the good.

Izzy shook her head sorrowfully at him. She reached up and brushed his tears. "It'll be okay, Dad," she said.

Dinosaurs had returned to the cruel Earth, but the planet's fate would not be determined by them. It would be decided by the cruelty and compassion of the Earth's current residents.

The wolf nestled his clutch.

PUNCTUATED EVOLUTION

New Profanity loomed over Dinosaur Falls National Wildlife Restricted Area, a sick mother watching over her broken family. Along her cliffs, Dimorphodons fought over scraps of a juvenile bald eagle.

A shadow passed overhead. The Dimorphodons quickly reacted. The cowered in the eagle's nest and remained motionless. They didn't look up because then the monster might catch a glimpse of their eyes. And why should they look up? They'd seen large shadows cast down from overhead before. The Quetzalcoatlus usually left them alone, but it wasn't uncommon for the world's largest flying machine to decide to eat smaller flying dinosaurs.

The shadow disappeared along the cliffs. The Dimorphodons chirped as they returned to their feast. A long muscle became the rope in a tug-of-war between the Dimorphodons. The meat was crucial to their survival.

This time, the shadow passed much faster, and without notice. If they had been able to look, they wouldn't have seen a Quetzalcoatlus, but something much more fearsome. Two giant eagle claws reached out of the sky and swallowed the dinosaurs.

***

The Allosauruses tried another attempt at the herd of Ankylosauruses, but the swinging clubs and plated armor were too much for them. It was time to bow out of the hunt. They roared their displeasure and walked away, keeping a devilish saurian eye on the lost opportunity.

The Ankylosaurus herd returned to grazing. There was a lot of calories to make up, and the day was long.

Something low and long loped through the tall grass. An Ankylosaurus noted the movement in the grass. The Ank weighed whether this new thing was a threat.

The grass swished rapidly back and forth.

With a swing of his bone-plated tail, the Ank warned this creature to beware hunting them.

The thing in the tall grass was too low to be struck by his club. The attacker ran underneath the threat and reached out with its fangs, slitting the Ank's throat. The dinosaur cried out and tried to push it off, but this new creature was tenacious and refused to let go.

The Ank gargled as blood splashed into its windpipe. The little creature ripped side to side, slashing again and again into its soft flesh. After thrashing about and flailing like a drunk man on fire, the Ank stumbled and submitted to its own mortality.

The rest of the herd could do nothing to stop this killer. How do you prevent a carnivore you cannot stomp or club? They countered it the way they always had. They simply moved away from the kill site and hoped to avoid the creature in the future.

The Allosauruses were opportunistic predators, though. They growled at the low creature in the ground. The thing did not stop gulping down meat from the kill. The Allosauruses approached.

Out of the grass charged a giant badger, as large as a German Shepherd. Six inches long, its canines were as long as a saber-toothed cat's. The creature was formidable, but still much smaller than the hunger pangs of an Allosaurus. The two giant meat eaters made a move to steal the badger's meal.

The badger plunged face-forward into the first Allosaurus, burying his elongated canines in the creature's belly, then cutting him open from ribs to cloaca. Before the giant Allosaurus could react, its hot bowels spilled into the snow.

***

The wolf shot down the mountainside's rough rocks. Ahead of him ran the Amargasaurus, a 20-foot long sauropod, a tiny Diplodocus that was head-to-tail less than half the length of an Apatosaurus. Unlike other sauropods, though, this one had two long spines running down the back of its neck. The narrow spikes were strong as a rhinoceros' horn but colored in bright red and green zig-zags that morphed into the reticulated pattern of the dinosaur's green-and-black skin.

The wolf kept looking to the neck spines. Their vibrant colors attracted his eyes. He had to concentrate to focus on the kill.

The Amargasaurus was surprisingly light on its feet for such an elephantine animal. He nipped on the dinosaur's heels, and it brayed its frustration. The wolf, as large as he was, was lucky that the giant didn't turn on him.

He snatched at the dino's left heel. It turned from the ridgeline and into the dark forest. The wolf slowed to a trot and approached. Aside from the crashing sounds of the Amargasaurus as it fled pell-mell through the trees, he heard nothing. Gentle susurrations. Leaves flittered in the space where the spike-necked giant had disappeared.

Then, mauling and ripping. Terrible screams. Thousand-watt vocalizations from million-year-old predators that should not exist. Then silence again.

The wolf sniffed the darkness and curled his lip. Shadows emerged from the dark. Shadow with sharp teeth and scimitars for claws.

Click, click, click, the claw went against the fallen tree trunk.

The wolf lowered his body.

Suddenly, two raptors sprang from the left and right. A third launched from ahead, straight for his throat.

The raptor nuzzled his throat.

"GrooAWRrrr!" purred the young Utahraptor.

The raptors smelled of their kill. They had done excellently. The pack would survive.

Warg thought proudly and smugly to himself how much smarter raptors were to the human pup. Raptors understood language immediately.

The wolf stalked dinosaurs in the restricted area, but he was not alone.

Photo by Sam Shepherd

Thanks for Reading

If you enjoyed Hunting with Dinosaurs, please leave a review on Amazon. Like most authors, I depend on reviews and word of mouth referrals of readers, so anything you can add would be greatly appreciated.

I am also the author of:

Terrible Lizard

Zombie Dog Series
Cadaver Dog (Book 1)
Dead Dog (Book 2)
Zombie Dog (Book 3)
Ghost Dog (Book 4)

Severed Press Books by Doug Goodman
Dominion
Kaiju Fall
Kaijunaut
Shark Toothed Grin
Wendigo Road
Backpacking With Dinosaurs
Mountain Climbing With Dinosaurs

My website is dgoodman1.wordpress.com. Feel free to email me at douggoodmannet@gmail.com. I'd love to hear what you thought of the book. I also give out Mojo prizes to anyone who finds a typo or edit. To get your own digital photo of the dog that inspired Murder, e-mail me the typo/edit you find. To sign up to be notified of new releases, giveaways, and other book news, check out my website.

In case you are looking for a few other ways to reach me…

Facebook: Doug Goodman
Twitter: @DougGoodman1
Instagram: douggoodman_writes or TexasGeekDad
Pinterest: douggoodman

CHECK OUT OTHER GREAT DINOSAUR BOOKS

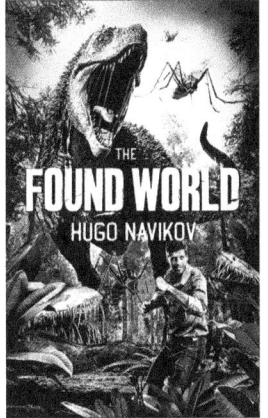

THE FOUND WORLD
by **Hugo Navikov**

A powerful global cabal wants adventurer Brett Russell to retrieve a superweapon stolen by the scientist who built it. To entice him to travel underneath one of the most dangerous volcanoes on Earth to find the scientist, this shadowy organization will pay him the only thing he cares about: information that will allow him to avenge his family's murder.

But before he can get paid, he and his team must enter an underground hellscape of killer plants, giant insects, terrifying dinosaurs, and an army of other predators never previously seen by man.

At the end of this journey awaits a revelation that could alter the fate of mankind … if they can make it back from this horrifying found world.

HOUSE OF THE GODS
by **Davide Mana**

High above the steamy jungle of the Amazon basin, rise the flat plateaus known as the Tepui, the House of the Gods. Lost worlds of unknown beauty, a naturalistic wonder, each an ecology onto itself, shunned by the local tribes for centuries. The House of the Gods was not made for men.

But now, the crew and passengers of a small charter plane are about to find what was hidden for sixty million years.

Lost on an island in the clouds 10.000 feet above the jungle, surrounded by dinosaurs, hunted by mysterious mercenaries, the survivors of Sligo Air flight 001 will quickly learn the only rule of life on Earth: Extinction.

CHECK OUT OTHER GREAT DINOSAUR BOOKS

PRIMORDIA
by **Greig Beck**

Ben Cartwright, former soldier, home to mourn the loss of his father stumbles upon cryptic letters from the past between the author, Arthur Conan Doyle and his great, great grandfather who vanished while exploring the Amazon jungle in 1908.

Amazingly, these letters lead Ben to believe that his ancestor's expedition was the basis for Doyle's fantastical tale of a lost world inhabited by long extinct creatures. As Ben digs some more he finds clues to the whereabouts of a lost notebook that might contain a map to a place that is home to creatures that would rewrite everything known about history, biology and evolution.

But other parties now know about the notebook, and will do anything to obtain it. For Ben and his friends, it becomes a race against time and against ruthless rivals.

In the remotest corners of Venezuela, along winding river trails known only to lost tribes, and through near impenetrable jungle, Ben and his novice team find a forbidden place more terrifying and dangerous than anything they could ever have imagined.

PANGAEA EXILES
by **Jeff Brackett**

Tried and convicted for his crimes, Sean Barrow is sent into temporal exile—banished to a time so far before recorded history that there is no chance that he, or any other criminal sent back, has any chance of altering history.

Now Sean must find a way to survive more than 200 million years in the past, in a world populated by monstrous creatures that would rend him limb from limb if they got the chance. And that's just his fellow prisoners.

The dinosaurs are almost as bad.

CHECK OUT OTHER GREAT DINOSAUR BOOKS

FLIPSIDE
by JAKE BIBLE

The year is 2046 and dinosaurs are real.

Time bubbles across the world, many as large as one hundred square miles, turn like clockwork, revealing prehistoric landscapes from the Cretaceous Period.

They reveal the Flipside.

Now, thirty years after the first Turn, the clockwork is breaking down as one of the world's powers has decided to exploit the phenomenon for their own gain, possibly destroying everything then and now in the process.

A MAN OUT OF TIME
by Christopher Laflan

Five years after the Chinese Axis detonated an unknown weapon of mass destruction off the southern coast of the United States, Special Ops Sergeant John Crider and the members of Shadow Company have finally captured what they all hope will lead to the end of the war. Unfortunately, the population within the United States is no longer sustainable. In an effort to stabilize the economy, the government enacts the Cryonics Act. One hundred years in suspended animation, all debt forgiven, and a chance at a less crowded future are too good to pass up for John and his young daughter.

Except not everything always goes as planned as Sergeant John Crider finds himself pitted against a land of prehistoric monsters genetically resurrected from the fossil record, murderous inhabitants, and a future he never wanted.